LOSING LOUISA

JUDITH CASELEY

Losing
Louisa

Frances Foster Books
Farrar, Straus and Giroux
New York

For my grandmother, Rebecca Cohen

Library of Congress Cataloging-in-Publication Data
Caseley, Judith.
    Losing Louisa / Judith Caseley. — 1st ed.
    p. cm.
    Summary: Sixteen-year-old Lacey worries about the effect of
her parents' divorce on her family, especially her mother, and about
her older sister's sexual activity, which may have made her pregnant.
    ISBN 0-374-34665-8
    [1. Divorce—Fiction. 2. Sexual ethics—Fiction. 3. Pregnancy—
Fiction.] I. Title.
PZ7.C2677Lo   1999
[Fic]—dc21   98-19501

LOSING LOUISA

1

❦

A few minutes past midnight, on Columbus Day to be exact, Lacey Monroe Levine heard muffled sounds coming from the basement. A thumping sound, an occasional metal *scree,* a low rumble that could be a voice. Her ear to the basement door, she began to reconsider her decision to finish the laundry, despite the fact that her gym clothes were lying wet in the washing machine and would probably smell of mildew in the morning.

Lacey wondered above the beating of her heart if she should wake her mother or drag her sister, Rosie, out of bed. Then the noises stopped abruptly, and the house was as silent as a tomb. She fled back upstairs to her bedroom. The laundry could wait.

Lacey grabbed an old trophy, the kind they gave to every kid who played sports in grade school, and clutched it to her chest under the covers. She lay still and waited.

For what, she had no idea. No new noises threatened the household. Where was the family mascot, anyhow?

"Here, puss puss," Lacey whispered, gripping the trophy with both hands as she paused to listen. "Sherman! Where are you, kitty?" Was her imagination playing tricks on her, or did she detect the sound of scratching? It occurred to Lacey that in her first round of laundry duty she might have trapped the poor animal in the basement. She crept out of bed, the trophy raised above her, whispering "Puss puss" at every third step and "Damned cat" as she reached the cellar door.

Lacey lowered her foot carefully onto the first step of the wooden stairway. "Sherman?" she whispered, cringing as the second step creaked under her weight. She clattered down the remaining steps as loud as she could, then rounded the corner to the washing machine. A cricket sped along the floor and disappeared.

The Levine basement had no fancy blond wood paneling like Lacey's best girlfriend Tony's had. It had no pool table, no bar with three stools perched in front of it, and no bathroom. It had not been turned into a recreation room for "the teenagers." The Levine basement housed three barrels full of outdated clothing (including an old pair of landlubber jeans from her mother's hippie days), a clothesline strung from corner to corner with wooden clothespins that held two pairs of underpants and a bra, a washing machine with congealed drips of blue detergent on top, and a clothes dryer. A do-it-yourself handbook on how to fix small appliances sat on top of a dusty coffeemaker.

4

When Lacey's parents divorced, her mother, Leonora, stopped using the coffeemaker. Every morning she boiled a cup of water in an old wedding present of a pot, poured it into a chipped "World's Best Mother" coffee mug, dumped in a spoonful of instant coffee, and drank it guiltily. She worked full-time at Herrick's Health Food Store, and Alfred Herrick, the owner, would not approve of her caffeine addiction.

A long fluorescent light suspended from the ceiling flickered above a cot, standing open and empty in front of the clothes dryer. Which was very strange, to say the least. Usually the cot was folded up, leaning against the wall, unless Leonora Levine's college chum Kris came for a visit, in which case they would drag it upstairs and stick it in the living room. Lacey had never seen it open in the basement before. A large flashlight sat upright on the cement floor next to it.

Lacey moved closer, training her eyes on a dark patch in the center of the mattress. She held out her index finger and gingerly touched the stain. It was wet.

"Shit," said Lacey, jumping back. She fled upstairs to the kitchen, rounded the corner, and took the second set of stairs two at a time, until she was safely back in bed. She tucked the trophy under her pillow, just in case.

A solid mass landed squarely on Lacey's stomach. She screamed so loud that the cat was startled into a fierce meow of her own. "Sherman!" said Lacey, hugging the animal to her. "You scared me to death!" Then she shifted her pillow so that the cat could lie next to her, purring in Lacey's ear until she finally fell asleep.

. . .

Lacey woke to the comforting sounds of morning. She turned lazily in bed, smiling as her mother serenaded her with a show tune from the shower. Lacey scooped up Sherman and scanned the floor for her slippers. "The heck with it," she muttered—it was her father who had always reminded her to wear them, and Michael Levine didn't live here anymore. Lacey padded barefoot, Sherman alongside her, past the bathroom and down the stairs to the kitchen. She reached the cellar door, took a deep breath, and pushed it open a crack. She inspected the eleven steps for signs of an intruder. Nothing. Sherman inched her nose between the door and the molding.

"My guard cat," whispered Lacey, bending to stroke her. "Where were you when I needed you?" She listened intently. "Is anybody down there?" she called into the opening, waiting for an answer as if a burglar might call back, "I'm getting ready to rob your house if you'd just let me get organized."

The first time Lacey had heard noises—almost a month ago, as summer was ending—her mother had said it was probably a cat in heat. Not their cat, but some other neighborhood cat. Nineteen-year-old Sherman, who had belonged to Lacey's father before he ever met Leonora, had aged into a fairly silent, dozy sort of feline who slept when the family slept, at the foot of the bed of her choice. Usually it was Lacey's.

Lacey moved quickly across the cement floor, the thin stream of morning light through the cellar window bolstering her courage. She leaned over the outstretched cot,

6

narrowing her eyes as she searched the mattress for the offending spot. She couldn't find it. It had dried and faded to nothing. Shrugging her shoulders, Lacey lifted the lid of the washing machine, reached in, pulled out a wad of damp clothing, and held it to her nose. Then she dumped the pile into the dryer, slammed the door shut, turned the dial, and pressed the starter button. The machine began to hum.

Upstairs, Lacey made a right turn into the foyer and swung open the front door. Eyes cast on the ground, she darted across the yard to retrieve the plastic-wrapped Glenwood newspaper. Most of their neighbors were older, but she would definitely not be happy if Kenny Lerner from down the street, Kenny who went to high school with her and liked to make up nasty rhymes about people, caught her outside in her pajamas. She would never hear the end of it. Lacey scooted back in, pausing briefly to shake the morning dew off the newspaper and to wipe her wet feet on the nubbly welcome mat.

She settled back into bed with the paper. Leonora had stopped warbling and was gargling now. Then Lacey heard her scrubbing her teeth with the nasty-tasting baking-soda toothpaste that made Lacey want to puke. Her mother spit once, rinsed, and muttered, "Happy birthday, Mr. Columbus."

"Talking to yourself, Ma?" Lacey called.

"To Christopher Columbus, honey," Leonora shouted back. "It's his birthday today."

"Afraid not, Ma. It's the anniversary of the day he came here to plunder America." Lacey waited for an answer.

"You always were smarter than me," yelled her mother.
Lacey grinned. "So how come you can't stay home to celebrate?" She hooked a leg outside and over her quilt, wiggling her toes at Leonora as her mother appeared in the doorway. "So what do you say, Ma? I heard noises in the basement again. It's downright creepy."

"You just don't want to do the laundry," said her mother. "Maybe it's the house settling. Or maybe it's that lazy lump of a cat, Lacey. Did you ever think of that?"

"It wasn't Shermie, Ma." Why get the poor old cat in trouble, thought Lacey, in case she wasn't responsible? "Hey, if our television set is gone when you get home from work tonight, don't blame me." Lacey watched as Leonora Levine unsnapped her snug black jeans and tucked her chartreuse blouse inside. Her mother had a tiny hill of a belly. Lacey smoothed a hand across the contour of her own stomach and sucked it in. It was flatter than her mother's. But then, she hadn't had two kids, as Leonora would point out, through unnatural childbirth. Her mother refused to use the word "natural" when it came to describing her pregnancies. Lacey shrank into a corner when she heard Leonora tell perfectly innocent strangers who happened to be pregnant that there was nothing natural about pushing a nine-pound baby out of your body.

Lacey wondered vaguely if she dared to tell her mother that she was getting too old to be wearing jeans with spandex in them. She wavered. Leonora's face was relaxed and worry-free for a change. Perhaps Columbus Day was not the day to give constructive criticism.

"I wish I could just stay home all day with you girls," said her mother. "But I've got a stack of bills to pay. Those teeth of yours are killing me."

"I inherited everything from you, you know," Lacey said grouchily. "It's not my fault I have bad teeth."

Leonora snorted, and leaned against the doorframe. "You have your father's lousy teeth, dear girl. His are pearly white and rotten. Mine are perfect. Not a single filling." She opened her mouth to display her molars.

"Please, Ma," said Lacey, making a face. "Anyway, yours are yellow, so I'm glad I have his."

"Too bad I have to pay the bills, though, isn't it?" said her mother, a flash of anger in her eyes.

"Can't you ask Dad for more money?"

"He says he's stretched to the limit," said Leonora. "Poor guy. New houses cost money." She turned to go. "Anyway, Mr. Livingstone needs his carrot juice, so I'd better get moving."

"Wait, Ma," Lacey called softly.

"What?" Her mother stopped in her tracks, arms motionless in midair as if she were playing red-light greenlight.

"You know why Mr. Livingstone comes in every day for his carrot juice, don't you?"

Leonora turned her head a fraction of an inch, enough for Lacey to see the curve of her cheek, the edge of a smile, and the spoon hanging from her left earlobe swinging back and forth. "Why?" she said.

"Because he has a crush on you, that's why. He lusts after your body, Ma."

9

Her mother's laugh rippled until she clapped a hand over her mouth. "We'll wake Rosie," she whispered, turning her head so that Lacey could see the fork dangling from her right ear.

"He does, Ma. I've seen him watch you." Lacey pulled her knees to her chest. "He practically drools when you're around."

"Mr. Livingstone is so old that drooling is a natural function," said Leonora, grinning. "Anyway, I think it's the carrots. He likes the sensuous way I feed those carrots into the juicer."

"At least he notices you. I've had a crush on David since school started, and he doesn't even know I'm alive."

"A whole month!" said her mother in mock horror. "Pack a carrot in your lunch, and crunch it suggestively in his ear or something."

"He sits with his buddies in the cafeteria. And he's not into health food, Ma. He eats meat."

"A crush on a carnivore! Even worse," said Leonora, laughing as she continued down the hallway. "I have to go to work."

Lacey began reading an article about graffiti in her hometown. A small group of Glenwood youths were defacing public property again, and it was costing taxpayer dollars to clean the filth off. Lacey wondered vaguely what had been written, and if it had been brushed on in that fancy flowery-lettered way, or spray-painted. Did girls do it? Could her older sister, Rosie, have written "Rosie Loves Joseph," in her best penmanship, on the wall of the courthouse? Lacey dismissed the thought. Too wild for Rosie, who wore plain cotton bras and boring panties, along with the requisite oversized turtleneck to cover the big breasts that Lacey envied. She wondered if Rosie's boyfriend, Joseph, liked them, or did he have to apply for a visitor's pass whenever he wanted to pat them behind their prison of a bra? Bespectacled Joseph was Joey to his mother, who called regularly on the telephone to see if "my Joey" was coming home for dinner. "It's lasagna tonight," she'd whine into the telephone. "My Joey's favorite." But Joseph never cared about the menu. He'd eat tofu hotdogs and whole-grain burgers and plain pasta with spaghetti sauce from a jar instead of Mrs. Panteleone's homemade extravaganzas. He would chomp contentedly next to Rosie, saying little, with an occasional jab at his glasses to push them back up the slope of his nose. A tad smaller than Lacey and a tad bigger than Rosie, Joseph was not Lacey's idea of a boyfriend. But she couldn't help admiring his muscles—the small swift movement of fork to mouth flexed several in his upper arm. In Lacey's eyes, it was Joseph's only talent, however dazzling.

"I'm leaving!" called her mother from downstairs. "I'll bring home tofu pizza for dinner."

"Again?" moaned Lacey.

"You always have my permission to cook something, you know," shouted her mother. "Don't let Rosie sleep all day. Now I'm really going." The door shut firmly behind her.

Lacey threw back the covers and stood up, stretching her long arms to the ceiling. She bent to pick up an unwashed pair of socks—the clean ones were in the dryer. She slipped them on and marched into the hallway, hesitating for a moment outside Rosie's doorway. Then she knocked and entered, without waiting for an answer.

"Have you been sleeping in the basement?" Lacey addressed the curve of body under the sprigged coverlet.

A lump at the bottom twitched, and Rosie muttered, "Why would I want to sleep in the basement?"

"I don't know." Lacey sat down on the end of the bed to squeals of protest. "The cot was open, Rosie. Don't you think that's a little weird?"

"You're sitting on my leg!" said Rosie, yanking the covers away from a face that matched her name. With her mane of golden curls, she reminded Lacey of Sleeping Beauty in a plain cotton nightgown. Sleeping Beauty was decidedly grouchy today.

"Leave me alone," Rosie complained. "I don't know anything about a cot, and it's a holiday, and I want to sleep in."

"Some people say Columbus was a racist," said Lacey. "He might have been brave and all that, but you wouldn't want to have known him if you were a Native American or something."

"So I won't bake him a cake." Rosie pulled the covers back over her head. "Now go away."

"Well, somebody has been sleeping in the basement, and I know it wasn't me." Lacey stood up.

"What is this, *Goldilocks and the Three Bears?*" snarled Rosie. "Get a life."

·   ·   ·

Lacey wandered into the kitchen and swung open the refrigerator door. Nothing appealed to her. Not the low-fat cheeses or the fat-free yogurts or the twenty different kinds of organic salad—the hummus, the tabbouleh, the wild rice with sun-dried tomatoes. Scrambled eggs and bacon, that's what she craved, but her mother was too damned health-conscious to even buy bacon. Lacey took a plastic bag of whole-wheat bread out of the cupboard, wishing fervently that it was white bread, and popped two slices into the toaster. She opened the refrigerator and took out the butter, which Leonora now permitted the family to eat. Butter was back in favor, now that margarine was getting a bad rep. Leonora always followed the findings of the latest scientific study.

Lacey picked up the telephone and dialed Tony. It rang three times, which was ominous, because Tony usually picked up cheerily on the first ring.

"What?" Tony growled into the phone.

"I woke you," Lacey said, rummaging in the drawer for a knife.

"Yeah, and I was dreaming about Scott and me in a hot-air balloon. Thanks for waking me up in the middle of the romantic part. What's that clanging noise?"

"Your wake-up call. I need some support from my friend. Someone's been sleeping in my basement. The cot is open, and there's a wet spot. I touched it."

Tony said, "Gross me out, Lacey! Maybe it was a snail or something. Doesn't a snail leave a wet spot?"

"We don't have snails, Tony. We have crickets. Anyway, snails leave a long disgusting trail, don't they?" Lacey shuddered. "Oh, yuck, I'm grossing myself out, and I was just about to ask you to dinner. Do you want to have tofu pizza at my house tonight? My mom's specialty. So I can look at you instead of at Joey's rippling muscles."

Tony made the sound of someone barfing. "I'll pass," she said. "The muscle in his brain could use a little exercise. Unless of course he's using his *downstairs* muscle."

"His downstairs muscle?" said Lacey blankly.

Tony laughed. "He's dating the Virgin Mary, so I wouldn't think so."

"Perish the thought," said Lacey. "I don't think they even make out."

"What you need is some fresh air," Tony announced. "Meet me at Jake's Deli after breakfast. Maybe Scott will be there." She sighed artificially. "Scott, my hot-air-balloon fantasy man . . . in the dream that *you* interrupted." Tony made a sniffing sound. "Gotta go. I smell my mom's pancakes cooking."

Lacey sighed. "Lucky you. My mom's at work already. No fancy breakfast at the Levine house!" She picked up her half-eaten piece of toast and felt a surge of anger at her mother, that over-the-hill teenager in too-tight jeans and spoon-and-fork earrings who couldn't earn enough money to pay for the dentist. Her father's face, like a flare in the darkness, appeared in her head. Funny, handsome Michael Levine was living an hour or so away in a ritzier neighborhood with his new pregnant wife in his new house with its sparkling white-tiled kitchen with red accents. Lacey was having whole-wheat toast all alone in a kitchen with faded blue-flowered wallpaper that curled at

14

the edges. Lacey hated blue. She tossed the dried remains of her breakfast into the garbage. "I'll see you at Jake's," she said, hanging up the telephone.

Lacey switched on the radio. Her favorite band, the Mickies, kept her company as she held her plate under the steaming water. She threw it into the dish drainer, glaring for a moment at the red-lipstick-imprinted mug her mother had left on the counter. Then she sponged off the table and returned to her bedroom, yanking open a dresser drawer. It was filled with a jumble of Aunt Bertha's cast-offs, sweatshirts with sequined flowers and heart-shaped pieces of felt appliquéd across the chest, designs that Lacey detested. She always inherited Aunt Bertha's old clothes, and she had become an expert at snipping off the offending decorations with the same scissors that her mother used to trim the tiny hairs that appeared on the mole by her lip. At least they were better than Rosie's preppy discards. Besides, Rosie needed more room for her boobs and less room for her behind. Lacey was just the opposite.

She slipped on a black sweatshirt with a purple heart in its center—she'd already removed the five surrounding stars—and teamed it with tight black leggings and work boots. Lacey stuck her hip out as she stood in front of the full-length mirror on her bedroom door. It was similar to what her mother had worn, but was a fairly acceptable outfit for a sixteen-year-old. Her legs looked long and slender above the slouchy socks and clunky boots. Forget the baggy-jean look. Too bad if she was out of step with the others. She moved her face closer to the mirror and smiled widely. Good skin on a long face that no longer looked thin as her cheeks rounded above a smile. A mass of chestnut hair, lips that were pink and full, a straight nose. Uncle Harry had told her that her smile was dazzling, but, then, Uncle Harry was nearly fifty and didn't really count. Her deepset hazel eyes were the feature that got the most compliments from her mother's small crop of relatives. Grandma Pearl told her that her eyes would get her into trouble. Lacey's mother laughed, and said that her mouth would.

Lacey put a layer of mascara on her eyelashes, a thin line of sable beneath them. She liked the smoky look it gave her—the face of a French singer, she thought, although she'd never been to France and of French music knew only the odd power of Edith Piaf singing "Je Ne Regrette Rien" through her mother's closed bedroom door. Judging by the album cover, she didn't particularly want to look like Edith Piaf anyway.

"Where are you going?" said Rosie, standing barefooted and tousled in the doorway.

"To Jake's Deli," said Lacey, glancing casually at her sister's breasts, which had a life of their own under the nightgown.

Zaftig was the way Aunt Bertha described Rosie, with an approving nod of her head, cupping and dipping her hands as if she were testing melons in the supermarket. The heavier the melons, the sweeter the juice, and Lacey suspected that her double-D-cupped aunt felt the same way about breasts. Despite the raised eyebrows, the winks, and the nudges in the street whenever Rosie and her breasts swung by, Rosie seemed oblivious to the attention she was getting. Lacey, however, was not. She was sick with envy, and clipped photographs from magazines of beautiful flat-chested women, sticking them in the back of her third desk drawer to gather dust. Those waiflike models were her heroines. Their tiny breasts were the small jewels that most resembled Lacey's.

"Who's meeting you at Jake's?" asked Rosie.

"Your breasts have got to weigh at least ten pounds each," Lacey said matter-of-factly.

Rosie was not amused. "You wish, stick legs," she said.

"It beats table legs," Lacey shot back.

"Have a nice day," Rosie said nasally as Lacey pushed past her. "You're going to freeze without a jacket."

Lacey ran down the steps and headed for the front door. "By the way," she shouted over her shoulder, "Mom's making tofu pizza for supper." Lacey gripped the doorknob and stood still long enough to hear Rosie's reply.

"Spare us," she heard her sister say before she let the front door slam shut.

2

♥

Lacey rounded the corner and headed toward Glenwood's stretch of businesses, past the post office and the drugstore, the flower shop with its miniature pond, the Chinese restaurant with its fake pagoda, and the pizza parlor with its hanging neon pizza pie. As she drew near Jake's Deli, she almost jumped out of her clunky work boots. David Potter was lounging against the deli wall, drinking coffee. Lacey lurched backward behind the beam outside the pizza parlor, her heart thumping as she hung her head forward in between her legs. She shook her head from side to side as if she were shaking the dust from a dust mop, and swung her head upright so that her hair tumbled around her shoulders in what she hoped was a beautiful tangle. Lacey cleared her throat and, praying that he hadn't seen her in the first place, loped toward the apple of her eye.

She had first noticed David in choir. Mr. Lenney had arranged his chorus so that the bass singers stood behind the altos, which placed David directly behind Lacey, her head just about even with his chest. Right from the start, his very presence had made her knees tremble. The sound of his voice had given her goosebumps. An accidental nudge had made her heart hammer, all of which had enhanced her singing voice and given it a certain tremulous vibrato.

She could detect every movement of his body as he tapped a rhythm on his thigh or waved hello to a friend. Sometimes she could smell his aftershave, which pleased Lacey no end. She liked the notion that he wanted to smell nice. It seemed grownup to her. Lacey remembered perching on the edge of the bathtub while her father shaved, and when he had finished rinsing the razor under hot water, he would unscrew a series of men's colognes and let her choose a fragrance for him.

David's only aroma today was a cup of coffee, steaming in his hand. A hank of hair hung over his wide forehead, bobbing in the breeze as he bent to sip the hot brew. Lacey wondered if David had stood that morning in front of a mirror, examining himself with a critical eye. Did he ever turn to his best friend, Kenny, and say, "Does my hair look sexier this way over my forehead, or combed back?" As if he had read her mind, David combed through his hair with his fingers spread. The lock of hair stayed back for a moment, then sprang forward. As Lacey moved closer, he lifted his coffee cup to his mouth again, hip and cool like a model in a TV commercial, except that David had his shirt on. And no supermodel would be caught dead in the pea-green jeans that David was wearing.

In the Levine family, Rosie drank coffee alongside Leonora, milky and sweet. Lacey had cleaved to her father's choice of beverage, drinking tall, cold glasses of milk for breakfast, lunch, and dinner. Milk and cookies had been her favorite childhood snack until Leonora started up at Herrick's and healthy fruit bars replaced Oreo cookies, soy milk took over for the kind that came from cows. Finally, Leonora had met Lacey halfway, allowing the purchase of watery skim milk.

As David looked up, the insouciant hank of hair tickling his eyelashes, Lacey concentrated on making her approach runway model, not eager schoolgirl; leggy, not hippie; windswept, not sloppy; a loping gazelle, not a lumbering hippo.

"Hey," she said nonchalantly, blushing instantly as her eyes met David's.

"Hey yourself," said David, lifting his cup toward her so that a splash of scalding coffee ran down his hand and Lacey heard him suck air through his teeth, in obvious pain.

"Did you burn yourself? It looks awfully hot," she said, wishing she could bite off her tongue, because of course he had burned himself, for heaven's sake, a blister was practically forming before her eyes. As David blew on the back of his hand, she wondered if she should tell him about the old lady who'd scalded herself with a cup of coffee and sued the hamburger joint where she'd bought it and got lots of money. But the moment passed, and David began drinking his coffee again. His eyes no longer connected with hers and she agonized over whether she should move away or just go home and slit her throat. Why couldn't she utter the funny sexy-meet-cute lines that movie stars spoke in their light comedies? Why couldn't she banter, for heaven's sake! She watched him take off the lid and blow lightly on the hot liquid, the mark on his hand a definite red color. She was utterly tongue-tied and longed for Tony's entrance. Tony always knew what to say.

"Have you seen my friend Tony?" she asked, shifting her shoulders against the wall next to David, not too close but not too far away.

"Tony who?" David took another sip of his coffee and grimaced. It reminded Lacey of the cowboys in the old Westerns, downing shots of whiskey and making those pained macho faces and then wiping a hand across their grizzled whiskers.

"Tony Gellerman. You know Tony. She stands next to me in choir."

"I don't even remember where you stand in choir," David said. "Choir sucks."

Lacey reddened for a second time. How could he not know where she stood, when he'd found her Swatch watch on the stand behind her and had handed it to her, saying, "Time stands still when you're around." She could hardly wait until choir had ended that day so that she could discuss the meaning behind his statement with Tony, ad infinitum, until Tony had declared at lunchtime,

"Okay, he thinks you're so beautiful that his heart stops beating whenever he sees you. That's what it means. Are you happy now, and can we eat lunch?"

"Don't be sarcastic," Lacey had said to Tony, but she had floated through the rest of the day.

"Hello!" said David, tapping her on the shoulder. "I said, how is your sister?"

"Rosie is fine. She's home now." Why did they have to talk about her sister? Did David have a secret crush on her? Lacey couldn't think of anything to change the subject, except perhaps for a remark about the weather. The weather was definitely out.

"She still going with Joseph?" David threw back his head and drained his coffee cup just long enough for Lacey to spot a huge red pimple on the underside of his chin.

"They've been going together since they were juniors." Lacey turned to peer inside Jake's. "I wonder if I should get something to drink." There, she thought hopefully, maybe we won't have to talk about Rosie anymore.

"I'll get us a coffee. I could use another cup after last night." He gave Lacey a meaningful look, as though she should know already what a bad boy he'd been. Lacey laughed nervously and followed David as he entered the store to a jangle of bells.

A young man wearing a backward baseball cap stood behind the counter replenishing a basin of potato salad. "Hey, guys, what can I get you?" he said, brandishing a spoon. "Miss Lacey?" he said, bowing over the utensil.

Lacey blushed for a third time, cursing herself. "I'll have a cup of coffee with two sugars and lots of cream," she said, hoping that two sugars would be enough to disguise the bitter taste and praying that David couldn't tell the difference between windburned cheeks and a blush. Who was this person behind the counter anyway, and how did he know her name? And why had she ordered this terrible brew?

"Hey, Rob. Another coffee, milk, no sugar." David took a worn billfold out of his back pocket and threw two one-dollar bills on the counter. "Keep the change," he said with a laugh.

Rob grinned and said, "I'll buy that Mazda I've been wanting." Lacey detected a rise in Rob's own color as she sipped her coffee, and she blurted out, "I'd like a Mazda of my own," as if she knew a Mazda from a Volkswagen.

"Cool car," said Rob, heaping macaroni salad into a bin.

"Full of cholesterol," Lacey said as she eyed the creamy salad, immediately horrified at how much she sounded like Leonora.

"What is, a Mazda?" David crossed his eyes and laughed again. "No, seriously," he added. "Pasta is good for you. Runners fill up on it before they do a marathon. You know, they have carbo parties."

"Not carbos loaded with mayonnaise," said Rob. "I like to run myself. Mayo definitely would not do the trick. Unless of course you like to run and puke." He gave Lacey a look of alarm. "Hope I'm not ruining your appetite or anything."

Lacey shook her head and smiled, grateful that he had agreed with her.

David snorted. "I wouldn't eat anything here that wasn't bagged or canned, anyway."

"Actually, the food here's pretty good," Rob said, smoothing a spoon over a bowl of rice pudding. "Jake does most of the cooking."

"Who made the coffee?" asked David, swallowing a mouthful.

"I did," said Rob. "I get here at five-thirty in the morning and open up."

"It's delicious." Lacey took another sip, trying hard not to wrinkle up her nose in disgust. Rob was watching her curiously, and she was not about to insult his coffeemaking.

David turned abruptly and exited the deli without a word. Lacey trotted after him, but not before she turned to give an awkward wave to Rob.

"Goodbye, Miss Lacey," he called. "Enjoy that coffee," he added, winking at her.

Outside, the wind had picked up and there was a sprinkling of rain. Lacey wished she had listened to Rosie about wearing a jacket. "I can't believe it's drizzling," she said, holding the Styrofoam cup against her for warmth. "The paper didn't say anything about rain." Damn it, she thought, I'm talking about the weather.

"It was drizzling last night." David yawned widely.

"What were you doing last night? You look exhausted."

David raised an eyebrow. "Well, ma'am," he started. "Kenny and Stan and Scott and me, we were naughty little boys, that's for sure. And Barbara and what's-her-face, too. Anything else?"

"Sorry," said Lacey hastily. "I didn't mean to pry. Do you mean Barbara Bank and her friend Sandy?"

David snorted. "You didn't mean to pry, but you keep on coming back for more. Yeah, that's them. Bank and her friend Randy Sandy."

"Is that what you call her?" Lacey made a checklist of the bad words that rhymed with Lacey. Basey, Casey, Facey, Gracey, Macey, Pacey . . . oh God, Racy Lacey! But they could hardly call her that, could they? Not after just one kiss with Charles Pincer in the front seat of his father's station wagon, when she wouldn't even let him feel her up. Unless of course he'd blabbed all over town. Or lied.

"That's not all they call her," said David. "What a ho. Bank is the one, though. A real babe. Kenny says he'd like to bank her fire."

"Bank her fire?" said Lacey. "Kenny would?"

David shrugged. "Who wouldn't? Hey, what's the name of that TV show my grandmother loves to watch? The one with the old-lady detective. That's who you remind me of."

"I have no idea what you're talking about," Lacey said huffily. Whoever he meant, she knew it wasn't good.

"Well, she's nosy," David continued. "That's all I know about her."

"What other nicknames do you have for girls?" Lacey asked, so horrifyingly fascinated that she stopped caring if he thought she was nosy. "Do they call Tony anything? Or me?"

"Tony? If she's the redhead I think you mean, they call her the Bone. They don't call you anything."

"What does 'the Bone' mean?"

"You don't want to know." David threw back his head

and laughed, revealing again the pimple that she or Rosie or Tony would surely have disguised with a skin-toned acne cream before they ever dared to leave the house. Lacey wished that the oozing blemish would make her like David less, but it barely seemed to matter.

There was a long silence and David shifted his weight from one leg to another. Don't leave, she prayed. Stay just a little longer. And out of her mouth popped "Do you think Christopher Columbus was a racist?" She pictured herself running back into Jake's, grabbing that stupid spoon from Rob, and hitting herself over the head with it.

David rolled his eyes and said, "Who gives a shit?"

Lacey felt like she'd been hit in the stomach. The morning had turned into a complete disaster. She was ready to drop her nearly full cup of coffee into the garbage can and say goodbye when David muttered, "This must be your friend Tony."

Relief flooded Lacey as she watched Tony jauntily cross the street. Lacey couldn't help smiling as Tony's cap of red hair swung back and forth like in a shampoo commercial, her raisin-black lips gleaming against the paleness of her skin. There was nothing remotely bony about her curvy friend, but it hit Lacey in a flash that boning was another word for "doing the dirty," and Lacey felt herself go cold.

"Hey, girl," called Tony, "have you got room for breakfast?" Tony seemed unperturbed that David rolled his eyes again, as if to say, "I'm a 'no breakfast' kind of person, and that's the only cool way to go."

"Coffee?" said Tony, eyeing the cup in Lacey's hand. "Since when do you drink coffee?"

Lacey widened her eyes and glared at her friend. Ten marks against Tony, she said to herself, but, then, Tony would never drink a cup of anything that she didn't like just because a boy she had a crush on had bought it for her. Tony's absolute heartthrob, Scott McGraw, had called her "witchy lips" the other day, and Lacey was sure that her friend would reappear with pale pink lip gloss on her mouth, but Tony continued to wear her favorite lip color, Black Narcissus.

Tony fished in her knapsack, a crush of silver bracelets jingling on her wrist. "I have something here for you," she said.

"Man," said David, taking hold of her laden hand so that twenty or so hoops and charm bracelets slid down her arm. "You sound like a dog. You know, you hear them coming by the sound of the chain around their neck."

"I like being chained," Tony said glibly, which shut David up and made him drop her hand. Lacey watched to see if her friend was blushing, but Tony continued, white-faced and black-lipped, to rummage through her pocketbook until she said triumphantly, *"Voilà!* For you!"

Lacey took the plastic bag Tony held out to her. "Wait," said Tony. "There's more." Tony then produced a fork and a napkin, and said, "I felt sorry for you, all alone with your toast on Columbus Day."

"What the hell is that?" said David, peering at the plastic bag. "Dog turds?"

"Pancakes. For my friend," said Tony, unperturbed.

"Want one? I put butter on them, but no syrup. I didn't want her to get all sticky."

"Weird," said David, shaking his head as he started walking away from them. "Very weird."

Tony waited until he was halfway down the street before she said a word. "Lacey," she whispered, "I know you think he's the cat's meow, but I have to tell you something."

"The cat's meow?" said Lacey, unfastening the twisty on the plastic bag.

"The bee's knees," Tony said, laughing. "You know. His shit doesn't stink."

"What?" said Lacey. "Tell."

"You're not going to like it," said Tony.

"Tell," repeated Lacey, gingerly pulling out a pancake with the plastic fork.

"I have this gut instinct," said Tony, shaking her head.

"That his shit doesn't stink?" said Lacey, squinting at the pancake.

"Oh, it does, sweetie, it *does.*"

"If you don't tell me, I'm going to stuff this pancake down your shirt." Lacey held a ragged edge of pancake threateningly in the air.

Tony's blue eyes gazed compassionately at Lacey's. "Honey," she said, "he's an absolute asshole."

"Do you think so?" said Lacey. "He bought me a cup of coffee."

"Lacey my love," said Tony. "Listen carefully. You hate coffee."

"I know." Lacey bit into the pancake.

"If he bought you a cup of rat poison, would you drink it?" Tony pressed her nose against the deli window. "Who is that cutie in there? Isn't he in chorus with us?"

Lacey nearly choked on her pancake as she started to laugh. "His name is Rob, and that must be how he knows me. No, I would not drink rat poison if he gave it to me. David, I mean."

"Besides," said Tony wisely, "he had a zit on his neck that made me want to puke."

Lacey laughed so loud that a pigeon sitting on the nearby garbage can flew away. "I saw it," said Lacey, gasping.

"And what's the story behind the green jeans?" continued Tony. "Did his grandmother buy them for him at the thrift shop? His mother shouldn't have let him out of the house."

"He said he didn't know where I stood in chorus," Lacey said dejectedly.

"He didn't know, my eye." Tony put her arm around Lacey's shoulders. "He's an asshole," she said sadly, "but you love him anyway, don't you?"

"The next time I see him," Lacey said with a grin, "I promise I won't drink rat poison for him."

"The next time you see him," said Tony, "tell him to get his boil lanced. Now eat your pancake, dear."

Lacey peered at Tony. "Smile," she said. Tony immediately complied and Lacey took her napkin and gently wiped a smudge of Black Narcissus from Tony's front tooth. "There," she said. "Lipstick on your teeth."

"Truth," said Tony. "That's what friends are for."

3

♥

Leonora was removing three steaming miniature tofu pizzas from the oven when the telephone rang. Lacey didn't have to ask who was calling. Her mother's face was lively, the crinkle of lines around her eyes springing into play as she spoke to Grandma Pearl.

"Yes, Ma, my chickadees are sitting down to dinner with me," said Leonora, ignoring the cheeping sound that Lacey made.

"On the contrary, Mother, Joseph is not gracing us with his presence at dinner tonight. No, I haven't heard if Michael's darling wife has had her baby yet. She'll be giving birth to a little piglet quite soon now, I hear. Yes, the girls heard me. Let me amend that, Ma. What do you get if you cross a dog and a pig? A piglet-puppy? They know their mother is a bitch and a raving maniac, don't you, girls?"

Lacey and Rosie nodded, smirking as they bit into their tofu pizzas. It was only recently that their mother could joke about "the blessed event," as Leonora liked to call it. Since the divorce, the girls had been appalled by their mother's shifting personality—litmus paper gone bad, according to Lacey, with her father doing the acid test. Leonora had run amuck, shifting from fury to depressed calm, rage to agitated sadness, hysterics to silence. Sarcasm was a welcome relief.

Disaster had descended just two years ago. Leonora's best friend, Nilda Vilar, had named that period in the Levine household "Hurricane Michael." Disaster relief and damage control were organized by the locals: Grandma Pearl, Aunt Bertha, and Nilda. Leonora's cleanup was almost complete, except for a little lingering debris—a lack of funds, a cynical outlook on life, and the determination never to trust another man again.

It had started with a television talk show. Leonora was a self-admitted talk-show addict who made no effort to reform. When Grandma Pearl told her that she was setting a bad example for her daughters, Leonora shrugged and said, "It beats drugs or alcohol, Ma. Or gambling. Alice Ramsay went grocery shopping the other day and when she got home not a stick of furniture was left in the house—she came over to borrow my folding chairs and bridge table. Herb had gambled it all away, and the kids had nothing to sit on. They had been eating pizza on the kitchen floor, for God's sake. Is it so terrible that Rosie and Lacey come home to talk shows?"

Leonora's mother was not convinced. She sucked hard

31

on her cigarette and drew the smoke into her lungs. "Don't you think I'd like to give up smoking?" she said. "I make myself sick, you know. My clothes smell, my breath smells. I'm a walking poison stick. Dr. Schwartz says that nicotine is one of the hardest drugs to beat. He should know," she added. "He smokes three packs a day. It's a terrible addiction. Ferocious!" Grandma Pearl beat her chest with her fists, a cigarette clenched between her knuckles. "My body craves it," she said. Grandma Pearl paused for effect. "So what drug is keeping you hooked on that television screen?"

Leonora bared her teeth, but it was not a smile. "Habit, Ma. Hey, maybe it's my own little addiction, huh? But I like it. I triumph over their disasters."

Grandma Pearl's eyes lost their fighting luster. "At least you exercise," she said. "You set a good example for the girls by exercising. The Governor of New York says you should serve by example."

Leonora laughed. "So now they worry about their weight. That's the example I set for them by doing fifty sit-ups and one hundred leg lifts a day. Lacey pinched her thigh the other day and said, 'If it's more than an inch, you're fat.' "

Grandma Pearl sighed. "So let them catch you reading instead. How about that?"

"Rosie reads until she's blue in the face." Leonora sounded huffy. "And some days Lacey can't wake up in the morning because she stays up so late reading. So do me a favor, Ma. Lay off."

Leonora awoke every morning to the sounds of a

honey-voiced announcer on the clock radio. She switched on the transistor radio in the bathroom and listened to the news as she brushed her teeth. She got her two kids and her husband dressed, breakfasted, and out of the house like a well-oiled machine, then turned on the TV and started making beds to the deafening sounds of the day's first talk show.

She had something to say about every psychologist and social worker on the air. "This one doesn't know her ass from her elbow," she muttered as the therapist suggested family counseling to a contestant. That's what Leonora called them, "contestants," pathetically vying for the dubious position of most screwed-up, most duplicitous, most eccentric case history on the show.

Leonora was never the type to sit on the couch and stare at the television screen. She hardly knew what the panel looked like, listening hard as she scrubbed floors or stenciled on walls or folded laundry. At lunchtime she allowed herself the luxury of sitting down with her cup of soup, blueberry muffin, and coffee to see what she was missing. She detested the therapist who got up and stood behind a weeping woman to squeeze her shoulder. "Why can't she stay in her seat like the rest of them?" she said to the TV. She especially hated the one she nicknamed Miss Fancy, a family counselor who prepared her body carefully for television viewing, dark lip liner glaring at the camera, eyelashes thickly fringed around eyes that Leonora claimed flashed dollar signs, a suit with an elaborately embroidered collar, a pair of big gold earrings and matching choker. "Communication is the key," Miss

Fancy crooned to the stone-faced potbellied husband. Leonora drained her coffee cup and flared her nostrils. "He knows how to communicate with a beer can, asshole. Get him to Alcoholics Anonymous." Leonora did not pull her punches.

When Lacey got home from school and started her homework, she was interrupted several times by snatches of her mother's earthy advice. "Dysfunctional?" Leonora snorted. "Miss Fancy says they're *dysfunctional!* Show me a family that isn't!" Lacey was used to it, like someone who could only study with the radio on.

The day Leonora Levine gave up talk shows, cold turkey, was a day like any other. Lacey had come home, grabbed a glass of milk, and settled her book bag on a chair by the kitchen table. "How was school?" her mother asked, as she always did, from the living room. "Fine" was Lacey's answer. Their ritual was in place, with snack and homework and conversation ticking away in an orderly fashion. Rosie was at cheerleading practice and Leonora was ironing one of her husband's pale blue dress shirts in front of the television set. She looked up occasionally, shaking out the body of the shirt and smoothing it over the ironing board. Lacey finished a page of math problems at the kitchen table and bit into a Granny Smith apple left over from her lunch bag before tackling geography. She heard the gentle thump of the iron, the fizz of steam, the flapping of a shirtsleeve. She took a second bite of the apple and smiled as her mother cried, "The woman is blind, deaf, and dumb!" Lacey heard nothing that she hadn't heard before. Then there was the sound of the iron slamming down on the ironing board, the television droning on through her silence.

"Son of a bitch," Lacey heard her mother say, so quietly that it was almost a whisper. Leonora methodically hung up the pale blue shirt, put the iron on top of the oven to cool safely, and folded up the ironing board. "All done?" Lacey asked, and Leonora replied, "No, I'm not done at all." Lacey watched curiously as Leonora rummaged in a drawer and pulled out a stack of papers held together by several rubber bands, seated herself noisily next to Lacey at the kitchen table, and sifted through papers until she came to the credit-card statements. She read first one, then another, and then a third before stopping, the single sheet of paper trembling in her hands, her nose an inch from the printed page.

"Aha," her mother had exclaimed, like a detective in a cartoon. "So this is what they mean."

"What?" Lacey put down her apple.

"Has your father ever bought you a leather jacket?" Leonora asked.

"No," said Lacey.

"Has he bought Rosie a leather jacket? A leather jacket from a place called Leather World?" Leonora flapped the paper in Lacey's face.

"No," Lacey said slowly, sensing somehow that the question had nothing to do with fashion.

"Have you ever seen your father wear a leather jacket from a place called Leather World? Do we own anything leather, except for the goddamned leather armchair that your goddamned father needed to watch his goddamned

Sports Channel?" Leonora practically spit the words out.

"No," Lacey said. "You're scaring me, Mom."

Leonora pushed back from the table and said, "I'm sorry, honey. It's okay." Then she walked back into the living room and sat down on the couch. She started watching, without eating or drinking coffee or ironing or sewing. "It's okay," she repeated, sitting forward on the edge of the banana-colored cushion, rapt with attention, eyes glued to the television screen.

Lacey remained at the kitchen table. She heard a woman talking about partners, and watching for changes in behavior. Lacey tipped back in her chair so that she could see what the woman looked like. A poodle cap of shiny red hair, a tight purple skirt that every once in a while the woman tugged on, much too short for a woman her age, in Lacey's opinion. A purple jacket with a big pink cloth flower that flapped when the woman moved. The woman sat straight-backed, knees glued together, neck arched like a ballerina's. It might have been Miss Fancy, but Lacey wasn't sure.

A list appeared on the television screen, and Leonora leaned so far forward that Lacey was afraid she would slide right off the sofa.

"Let's go over the signs again," Miss Fancy continued. "Number one. Is he dressing differently? Is he sprucing up for work more than usual? Number two. Has he bought new underclothes? Has he switched from boxer shorts to bikini underwear? Changed his aftershave? Number three. Is he doing something very different in bed? Number four. Is he easily distracted? Does he run out of the house for milk or cigarettes or aspirin, some excuse, on a daily basis? He's probably calling her from a pay phone. Number five. Has his behavior changed? Is he very nice to you in an unusual way? That's the guilt working. Or is he extremely short with you, more than usual? That's the guilt, too—he can blame the affair on how badly you get along. Number six. Have his hours at work changed? Is he away from home in the evening, when he never used to be? Does he suddenly have business trips when he never took them before? Number seven. Has he made any unusual purchases that you haven't seen, flowers or jewelry, or some article of clothing that you haven't been given, particularly lingerie? Checking his credit-card purchases or your telephone bill for unusual calls can show a lot."

The talk-show host started shaking her head. "My goodness," she exclaimed. "I'd hate to snoop into my partner's things to find out something like that. It shows so little trust. And if you don't have trust in a relationship, what do you have?" The audience began clapping.

Miss Fancy spoke sharply and the applause died down. "Trust is lovely," she began. "Trust is wonderful. But would you rather have trust over the *truth?* Would you prefer everybody else knowing that your husband is sleeping around—your hairdresser, your grocer, your husband's secretary, and your best friend? That everybody, except for you, *stupid, trusting* you, has seen him with that blond bimbo from the video store? And isn't it your money, too, that he's spending with his credit card? Didn't you help him save to buy a house, didn't you have children together? Didn't you leave your great job and get pregnant and get fatter every year? Don't you deserve *more?*" Finally the expert had held out her hands, as if she were the Pope blessing the people. "Just let me say this," she said. "When I first looked at my husband's bills, I felt awful. My poor husband, how could I mistrust him, how could I violate his privacy? So I peeked, just a little. And do you know what I found? He'd bought her a *car.* A snazzy little sports car, the kind he wouldn't buy me in a million years because it wasn't practical with the kids and all. It was like every light in my head went out when I saw that, except for one tiny little light that got brighter and brighter. The light of discovery. The light of truth. And when I finally questioned him, can you guess what he said? You're imagining things. You're neurotic. You're downright nuts. Until I showed him a picture that the detective had taken of the bimbo and my husband, slobbering all over each other in a snazzy little sports car. So. Here I am, divorced, happy, and driving my own little sports car! There is life after divorce!" The audience went wild then and the lip liner shot a fist into the air, smiling broadly like a prizefighter who'd won. The talk-show host nodded her head as though she'd been in agreement all along, and switched to a commercial break.

Leonora stood up and walked over to the television set. A beautiful woman lay dreamily in a bathtub, immersed in bubbles. "No one will ever know" flashed across the screen, then the name of a feminine hygiene product.

"Why don't you go slit your wrists," Leonora said grimly, jabbing at a button so that the image faded. She remained standing, shoulders slumped, the reverse image of the straight-backed ballerina-therapist-expert lady who had just ruined her life.

"Lacey," Leonora said.

"What, Mom?" Lacey wondered if her mother could hear the fear in her voice.

"I said yes to practically every one of those questions. Yes, yes, yes, yes." She was still facing the empty screen of the television set.

Lacey picked up her apple. A line of brown had started to form around the edge of the white flesh. "I don't understand," she said mildly, as though her math homework was giving her problems.

"I don't, either," said her mother. "But I don't own a leather coat and neither do you." Then she turned and walked out of the room.

When Michael Levine came home that evening, he'd walked into the eye of the storm. Leonora was still and silent. She handed him a plastic-wrapped suit that she had picked up at the dry cleaners, poured him a glass of seltzer when he complained that he was thirsty, gave him the newspaper when he sank down into his favorite leather armchair in the spot where the late-afternoon sun trickled in through the lace curtains. "Ahhh," he sighed. "It's good to be home."

Lacey watched with hooded eyes as her mother performed robotic wifely chores. She thought it odd that her father never noticed that the television set was off. She thought it odder still that he didn't perceive her mother's silent bubbling anger. Leonora avoided looking at Michael Levine in any way, shape, or form. She shrank from him when he passed her, kept their fingers from touching when she handed him his glass or took it away. When he mentioned a new action movie that had been well reviewed, she said, "I don't give a shit," with such contempt that he looked startled. "I thought you might like it," he commented mildly before he went on to mention that his secretary thought he resembled the lead actor. Leonora replied, "Around the jowls."

"Around the jowls?" said her husband, hesitation in his voice. "Around the jowls?" he repeated, patting the lower portion of his jaw with his fingers. His eyes sought Leonora's. Finally, he said, "That's not good, Lee," in the injured voice of a five-year-old. "That's not good at all. I wonder if that's what Ellie meant."

"Ellie?" said Leonora. "Is that her name, Michael? Ellie? Then this must be hers!" She balled up the credit-card summary, scrunching it hard in her hands until it was round and tight, and threw it at him. It hit the edge of his cheek before skimming across the floor.

Lacey's hand moved to her chest as her heart thumped into overdrive. Michael Levine's face drained of color. "I'm so sorry, Lee," he said faintly.

Leonora looked as though she had been punched. Miss Fancy had cautioned that he'd say she was neurotic. Imagining things. Downright nuts. But Michael Levine had caved in immediately. He had never denied a thing. Miss Fancy was dead wrong.

Leonora rallied quickly. "Bullshit!" she said, with much more force than Lacey had ever even seen her use at a talk-show contestant. "If you were so sorry, why didn't you walk the other way?" Tears were running down her face now. "That's what we always promised each other," she said, swiping at the wetness on her cheeks as if it were the enemy. "That when the grass looked greener, Michael, we would walk the other way."

Over the next few days, Lacey's mother erupted into a series of furious soliloquies aimed at her husband, with no need for a response. She flip-flopped from screaming and crying to days of total silence, hushed telephone calls, more pleading and wailing, hours of clipped conversation in the privacy of their bedroom. Michael Levine's behavior was close to saintly. He ducked when Leonora tossed, looked mournful when she accused, played dead to her desperate lunges. Lacey overheard her mother ask him, "What is it that she has that I don't have, Michael? Is it the body? Is it the newness of it all? The flush of young love?" Her father's voice was level when he replied. "It's not new, Lee. We've been together for two years." After that, every time a door slammed, Lacey imagined that her father was leaving for good.

Early one morning, she heard a thumping down the stairs and the click of the front door that in her sleepy coherence Lacey knew was her father's final exit. She ran down the stairs three steps at a time and felt the flutter of paper at her feet. Three tags lay scattered on the carpet, airport luggage tags ripped from her father's suitcases. She knew he was gone.

Lacey and Rosie and their mother ate breakfast in silence. Leonora picked up the phone on its first ring and said, "Coward," bitterly into the receiver before handing it to Rosie. Rosie nodded into the telephone, telling her father yes, she knew that the divorce was not her fault at all, yes, she realized that things had been rocky for a while, no, she wouldn't hate him forever. She handed the receiver to Lacey and sat there, staring at her waffle. Leonora listened intently, wiping the same section of counter with a rag, polishing six inches of surface until it gleamed.

"I understand, Daddy, it's okay. Thank you, Daddy," said Lacey, her voice hushed in the still kitchen. She hung up the receiver gently.

"What the hell are you thanking him for?" said Leonora.

"For Sherman. He's letting us keep the cat. He knows how much we . . ." Lacey cleared her throat and corrected herself. "He knows how much I love her."

"Wonderful," said her mother. "He gets the slut of a secretary at work, and we get to keep the cat. One more mouth to feed. We get to keep the frigging *cat.*"

Lacey cried for the very first time then, a torrent of tears that slid down her face and dropped like rain onto her waffle. Rosie sat dry-eyed until her face suddenly crumpled and she balled up her fists and jammed them into her eyes and started crying alongside her sister. Leonora bent low over the counter. She put down her rag, turned, and hooked one arm around Lacey's neck and the other around Rosie's, crushing them together. "I'm sorry, girls," she whispered. "So sorry."

Grandma Pearl arrived with suitcases, although she

lived only about twenty minutes away. Pots of chicken soup simmered in the kitchen as if the whole family had come down with the flu. The soup and cigarette smoke and air freshener were the new smells in the Levine household.

Lacey was doing homework in the kitchen when she heard her mother cry out, "How can I ever survive?" Grandma Pearl's voice was coffee-stained and raspy as she dispensed advice. She took her daughter's hand and looked straight into her eyes and said, "Are you going to let a man ruin your life, a man like him?" with so much venom that it took Lacey by surprise.

Leonora sounded equally astonished. "I thought you liked him, Ma," she said. "You said he was like a son to you!"

Grandma Pearl laughed. "That was then, honey," she said. "This is now."

That night they all watched television together and Leonora cried at the sad parts, Grandma coughing and patting and soothing. "Girls," she said to Lacey and Rosie, "your father made a mistake. He screwed around, he broke up the family. That's terrible," she told them. "But remember that he loves you. I know he does." She turned to Rosie. "When you were born, your father was the one who said you were his little rose. Remember, Lee?" Leonora had nodded in misery as her mother continued. "He said your lips were like rosebuds, Rosie, and they were. No one could argue. And your mother said, 'But Rose is such an old-fashioned name, worse than Leonora. Remember, Lee Lee?" Leonora had smiled, a wobbly smile, and Grandma Pearl said, "I even gave him hell, you know, don't saddle a child with a name like Rose. I had the name Pearl, and I've always hated it. At least your mother was named after my sister who died. She fell out of a tree and broke her neck, a terrible thing." Then Grandma Pearl had turned to Lacey and said, "And you, my Lacey. Your father was so in love with you! He thought you were the most enchanting baby he had ever seen, and my sister, Bertha, had given you this beautiful embroidered gown, *goyische* almost, like a christening gown, with lace all over it, and your mother dressed you in it and your father picked you up and said, 'Lacey. She's so beautiful she has to be called Lacey.' "

Leonora had laughed then, a strangled kind of laughter, and spoke for the first time. "That's when I got the name Monroe in there, honey. I always thought that Marilyn Monroe was the most beautiful star of them all. I cried for days when she died. So we called you Lacey Monroe Levine. I hated the name Marilyn, or I would have called you that."

Grandma Pearl had patted Lacey on the knee and said, "Bertha, the one who gave you the *goyische* gown, she said it was a crime that your name was a Christian name. Go figure. She dresses you like a little Christian angel and she complains about the name. She said Monroe was like that President, James Monroe, very hoity-toity, and what kind of Jew was Lacey?"

Then Grandma and Leonora and Lacey and Rosie had started to laugh, in spite of themselves, and Grandma had shut off the TV and lit another cigarette.

Soon after that, when Grandma Pearl felt that she had cajoled and counseled her daughter into the land of the living, which to Lacey meant that her mother actually put on lipstick and combed her hair again, Grandma took her suitcases and left. But not before she called her friend Max from the Senior Citizens Center. "He knows everybody," Grandma informed them. "Owns three Cadillacs and wins at bingo every week. So what does he do in his spare time? He collects soda cans and hands them in for the nickels. Can you imagine? He has a screw loose. But that's how millionaires are made, Lee. They're all *meshuggeners.*" But Max Mandel was a *meshuggener* who knew a man who owned a health-food store nearby, and that's how Leonora Levine switched from feeding Michael Levine steak to feeding her daughters meatless hotdogs and tofu pizza.

4

♥

The year that Michael Levine left home for good, Leonora was not the only one in the family who got a job. Lacey and Rosie had babysat before, on occasion, but they began doing so in earnest when they discovered their mother's iron grip around the family purse strings. In the beginning, Rosie got most of the jobs because she was older and had more connections. Her sister got the leavings. Lacey felt a little like the Victorian girls in historical novels who had to wait until their older sisters got married before they could become engaged themselves.

Leonora had never been in charge of the major bills before, and despite the fact that Michael Levine was responsibly paying his court-ordered share without a fuss, she was totally overwhelmed. Money was definitely scarcer. The day Leonora wrote out a check for their first electric bill as a family of three was the day she began nagging the girls to turn out the lights when they left the room, to switch off the television if they weren't watching. The water bill sent Leonora on a shower-shortening regime, and the dishwasher was declared off-limits. The cable-television bill was paid the first month, the subscription canceled the next, over the wild protestations of the girls. "Watch network," was their mother's stony retort, "or read a book."

Some evenings, while Lacey did her homework, her mother sat next to her, rifling through a stack of papers and muttering to herself about car insurance and mortgage payments and what the hell was Blue Cross Blue Shield for if it didn't pick up the medical bills? When Michael Levine had handled the family finances, Lacey could remember her mother talking to Aunt Bertha in Florida for as long as it took to watch a television show, longer even. Now, *It's long distance* or *You've been on long enough* floated through the air whenever somone made a call. Lacey hated it. She also hated the slight puckering of her mother's mouth as though she were sucking on a lemon after eating sugar, as Leonora made neat stacks of papers in order of paying importance.

Secretly, Lacey thought her mother never looked uglier than she did when paying bills, with one exception . . . when she was helping Lacey or Rosie with their math homework. No puckering then, no crease in the forehead. Her face merely hardened into a hostile mask until Lacey's dull, uncomprehending façade pushed her mother right over the edge. Leonora sometimes stalked out of the dining room only to execute a furious dance in and out of the room to check on her daughter's progress. Lacey's fist-pounding on the table accompanied by "I still don't get it" made Leonora scream so loud that the "Have you hugged your child today?" advertisements on the television later made her wince in pain. Once she swatted Lacey over the head with the math book, put her head down on the kitchen table, and bawled. Lacey found herself comforting Leonora. "It's okay, Ma. It didn't really hurt," she said, trying to quell her mother's crying.

"I will never do that again," Leonora promised later, when she came in to say good night to Lacey.

"I hate the swearing more," Lacey said blandly, but she accepted her mother's hug and turned over to go to sleep.

If Lacey wanted a particular pair of designer jeans, or Rosie had her heart set on a preppy little shirt with a horse galloping across its pocket, the girls no longer bothered telling their mother. Leonora would most likely have raised one eyebrow or curled a part of her lip at them, their mother's version of "Get real, girls." After Rosie met Joseph behind the counter at his father's dry-cleaning shop, she started babysitting on Friday nights and seeing Joseph on Saturdays. Some nights, when they went to the movies at the Mall, Rosie came home with more than just a ticket stub: a shirt, a scarf, a belt. Rosie blinked, and Joseph bought.

Lacey was incensed. "It would take me four Saturdays in a row to buy what Rosie is wearing on her back right now," she complained bitterly.

"She gets them cleaned for free, too!" said Leonora. "There's no justice in this world."

"I'm not kidding, Ma," Lacey said.

"Get a boyfriend of your own," Rosie said blithely.

"I wouldn't take stuff from my boyfriend the way you do. You're a leech!" Lacey cried indignantly. "You're a . . . kept woman," she added hesitantly.

"A kept woman?" said Rosie, rolling her eyes at her mother. "You don't even know what that means."

"A kept woman," said Leonora, "is what I was when I was married to your father. Except that I didn't get the money, the clothes, the jewels, or the car. I got the housework, the aggravation, and the dropped uterus . . ." She paused. "And the divorce."

"A dropped what? Gross me out, Ma."

"A kept woman is a dependent woman." Leonora softened. "I want you girls to go to college. Find a job that gives you satisfaction. I met your father when I was a sophomore at Penn State. I married him the following summer. Said I'd finish school later. What was I afraid of, I ask myself. Having a life of my own? That's why I want you and Rosie to have a career, make a good living for yourselves."

"She's found a boyfriend instead," said Lacey, jabbing a finger at Rosie. "I have to get everything I need by myself."

Leonora snorted.

"It's true!" said Lacey vehemently.

"I see!" said Leonora, her voice as trickly as honey. "But you will let me pay for things like shoes and socks and dental bills, won't you, dear?"

It took Lacey only a moment to detect her mother's

not so subtle brand of post–Michael Levine sarcasm. "Dad never once complained about paying for anything we needed," Lacey declared. "Besides, he sends you money, doesn't he?"

Leonora lashed out: "Money? Sure, Dad sends me money. But sending money is not staying home from work because one of you girls is sick, is it, Lacey? Dad never once made your lunches either, or helped you with your schoolwork unless I forced him into it, or knew when the hell a Girl Scout meeting was, did he, Lacey?"

Lacey stayed quiet, preparing to launch her missile assault. "He helped us with math," she said. "You're terrible at math. Rosie and I are going to flunk out because of you."

Lacey waited for her retort, but none came.

Finally, Rosie said, "What's a dropped uterus, Ma?"

Her mother raised her head haughtily. "I'm not telling," she said. "You'll just have to find out for yourself."

A few weeks later, Lacey posted a handwritten notice in Herrick's Health Food Store, looking for a steady babysitting job. Lacey gave up Saturday nights in the name of money.

Tony was horrified when she found out. "Every Saturday night? How am I going to walk into Simone's house when she has one of those parties where the boys are invited? What am I going to do, waltz in there by myself?"

"Can't you go with Caroline?" Lacey ventured.

Tony fixed Lacey with a withering stare. With her Black Narcissus lipstick that in the early days she applied as soon as she left the house, she had a look of pure malevolence. "Caroline?" she said icily.

"She's not so bad," said Lacey. Caroline was a half pint of a blonde that Tony and Lacey had met in Art Club. Her eyes were huge blue crystal saucers that Caroline had emphasized by fringing them with navy-blue mascara. Tony had immediately asked her if she was wearing contact lenses. "They even beat Mel Gibson's eyes," she'd gushed. "Don't they, Lacey?"

Lacey couldn't remember what Mel Gibson's eyes looked like, but she had volunteered, "They remind me of Paul Newman's."

"He's kind of old," said Caroline hesitantly. "But I'm not wearing contact lenses." She blinked innocently. "My father has the same eyes."

Tony had exchanged glances with Lacey. This new piece of information meant that the darting motion of Caroline's pupils, like the quick flicker of minnows in a pond, was not the result of the presence of a foreign body in her eyes.

"She's like a scared rabbit," Tony whispered later to Lacey.

"It looks like a tic," Lacey whispered back. "My cousin Robert had one when he was little. His eye twitched when he was nervous."

Shy Caroline was thankful for their friendship. Her eyes stopped twitching long enough to brighten when the duo entered the art room, and the three of them shared paint pots and paper as Mr. Harmon gave them instruction.

"Oh, just what I want to do, take Scared Rabbit with me to a party," Tony continued. "Maybe I can learn that trick of hers . . ." She copied Caroline's flickering eye movement to such perfection that Lacey couldn't keep herself from laughing.

"You're so cruel," she said, giggling, which only spurred Tony on.

"We can go as twins!" she said. "I'll put on that little headband with the bow and pale pink lipstick and we can twitter our eyes together. We'll be such a hit!"

"That headband isn't so bad," Lacey said in between bouts of laughter. "Rosie has one like it."

"Ohhhh! Rosie, Miss Prep, wears one. Well, don't you think you should get one, too, and we'll all go out for pizza on Friday night, the four of us? Four Nerds in a Headband," said Tony. "Sounds like a bad movie."

Lacey spent Friday nights exclusively with Tony. Leonora accused them of roaming. "It's just hanging," Lacey told her mother. Friday-night loitering, as some of the shopkeepers called it, felt much safer to Lacey than the high-pitched doings of the following night. She was happy listening sympathetically to Tony's Saturday-night dilemmas. Should she go to Sal's bowling party or Randy's girl/boy birthday party? Would it help to have Caroline along for the ride, or would Caroline hold her back?

Munching on pizza, Lacey advised her to take Caroline. "There's safety in numbers," she told her friend.

"That's why I need you there," Tony said glumly.

When they finished their pizza, they hung out with

friends in front of Jake's, purchasing a soda or two to reserve the right to stand there. Some nights Rosie came along with Joseph and they would walk Lacey home. By then, Rosie had stopped babysitting altogether.

Bob and Karen Drew had one darling little toddler named Jason and several bedside parenting books to help them raise him. Leonora had the chance to examine the couple firsthand as she watched them scan Lacey's notice on the Herrick's bulletin board. NEAT, RESPONSIBLE GIRL, LOVES CHILDREN, SEEKS STEADY BABYSITTING JOB. MATURE AND CARING. CALL 676-4529 OR SPEAK TO LEONORA BEHIND THE JUICER. Leonora was a converted vegetarian by then, trusting herbivores over carnivores, and she knew Karen Drew by the benign contents of her shopping cart. It was Leonora who'd told Lacey to add the phrase "loves children." "Don't use the word 'kids,' " she cautioned. "Some people think it denigrates children."

She approved of Karen and Bob Drew, but cautioned her daughter. "Watch out for the mother. She told me she loves him more than life itself."

"What's wrong with that?" Lacey had asked.

"We all feel like that, especially when they're babies. But Karen Drew has a smile on her face when he wrecks my whole display of vegetarian baked beans, honey. He can do no wrong."

"So he's a brat," said Lacey.

"He's too young to be a brat," Leonora said, sniffing. "But just wait."

On the debut evening of Lacey's babysitting job, Karen Drew motioned for Lacey to sit down next to her on the once white couch in the living room. It had turned oatmeal-colored during the twenty months that Jason had graced the world with his presence, but Lacey could still see the original color from the edges of the cushions. Mrs. Drew quizzed Lacey on her child-care techniques, which were practically nil. Lacey lied. She pretended to be amused when Mrs. Drew asked her if she knew how to change a diaper. By all means, Lacey told Karen, show me your method of holding a bottle so that the air bubbles don't make the baby sick. No objects of any kind in the outlets, that's understandable.

At last, when Mrs. Drew was satisfied that Lacey knew the rudiments of babysitting, she handed her a sheet of paper. In red felt-tip pen across the top of the page, Karen had written:

How to Put Jason to Bed

1. Say to him, it's time for your milky. Put him on your lap and give him his milk bottle.

2. Read him four books. He may choose them if you hold them out to him.

3. Place him in his crib with his two blankies, the duck one and the blue one. Give him his pink pacifier, the one that looks like Miss Piggy.

4. Sing him the song from *Guys and Dolls,* "I Love You, a Bushel and a Peck." If you don't know the words, I'll write them down for you. You can always get the tape out of the library.

5. Leave the room. If he cries, return and check to see if his pacifier has fallen out of his mouth. If it has, find it for

him and put it back in. If not, rub his back with a circular motion. Take him out of the crib only if he is screaming. Rock him up and down and return him to the crib with his blankies and his pacifier.

6. Try not to give him more milk. Under no circumstances are you to give him a bottle in bed. It rots the teeth.

Karen had gone over the list, step by step, while twenty-month-old Jason toddled rings around them. Luckily, Lacey knew the words and tune to the *Guys and Dolls* song. She gave Karen a practice run, and Karen nodded approvingly. Then Bob Drew appeared, reminding Lacey to remove the plug from the outlet if she should decide to make microwave popcorn that evening, and not to open the door to strangers. He cleared his throat and asked her if she had a boyfriend. "Nobody steady," she told him. "No visitors are allowed," he informed her. No fear of that, thought Lacey, wondering if he knew that she was only fourteen. She took the telephone number that Mr. Drew handed her. "Call us if you have any problems," he said, ushering his wife out of the apartment.

It was only after their departure that Lacey noticed a decidedly putrid smell coming from Jason's diaper. It occurred to Lacey that perhaps lying about knowing how to change a diaper was a mistake.

Lacey called her mother.

"So they left you a package," said Leonora, laughing into the telephone. "Just read the directions on the box, honey. It's very simple."

"I'm not making soup here, Ma," complained Lacey. "I

55

have a squirming child in front of me who won't lay still. I have a penis here, Ma. What if he pees in my face?"

"You wipe it off." Leonora laughed some more. "We're talking tape, honey, not safety pins like in the old days. Stick him on the clean diaper, tape the thing together, and you're done."

A telephone call later, Lacey screamed into the phone, "There's disgusting stuff all over his bottom, Ma. He's covered."

Leonora sighed. "Find the Baby Wipes and clean him off. Is he lying on the floor? Don't let him roll off the table."

"Hold on, Ma," said Lacey, putting the receiver down on the carpet and running after the small naked body, with its protruding brown behind, which was heading for the living room. She grasped him under the armpits and held the squirming little boy at arm's length. Somehow she managed to get him back down on the bedroom floor with a box of Baby Wipes. Lacey held her breath as she gingerly wiped the baby.

"I think I'm going to puke!" she shouted toward the telephone. Lacey had to hope that Mrs. Drew kept a hidden supply of Baby Wipes, as she used them with abandon, until the box was empty. She had succeeded in wiping Jason's butt totally clean when she noticed a stripe of bright red running down his crack. "What's the matter with him?" Lacey picked up the telephone and asked her mother, who was defrosting the refrigerator with the phone cradled between her ear and her shoulder. "He's beet red around the butt!"

"He has diaper rash." Leonora no longer sounded

amused. "Find the cream called Balmex or Desitin and rub it on the red part."

"Already I'm not getting paid enough for this job," Lacey snarled into the telephone as she emptied out a bucket of baby paraphernalia and found the proper ointment. She sucked in her breath and, bending the baby's pliable legs back over his head so that his behind was prominently displayed, smeared a liberal amount of cream on the red stripe. Jason kept busy by chewing on a soft rubber ball. Lacey ruined a third diaper by twisting its tapes together. She tried not to picture the possible headlines: NAKED BABY WITH DIAPER OINTMENT ALL OVER HIM FOUND CHOKING ON BALL. LIAR OF A BABYSITTER GETS LIFE IMPRISONMENT. The baby had other ideas, however, as he bounced the rubber ball off Lacey's forehead and flipped over. Lacey tackled him and, with gentle pressure from her right knee, managed to diaper him backward. "Goodbye, Ma," she whispered into the telephone. "I'm exhausted. I'm ready for bed now."

"But is he?" said her mother, chuckling as she hung up the phone.

He wasn't. List in one hand and baby hoisted over her shoulder, Lacey crooned, "Would Jason like his milky?"

"No," said Jason emphatically.

"But it's bedtime," said Lacey, scanning the piece of paper as she deposited the baby onto the couch. She scooped up a handful of books and threw them next to Jason. "Pick, honey." Jason scrambled off the couch and sat down next to a house made of blocks. With one swipe of his sturdy little hand, he sent the cubes flying.

Lacey spent the next ten minutes retrieving blocks

from under the couch and behind the china cabinet and settled down to building Jason another house, which he abandoned immediately for the marble run, a mass of connecting tubes and runways that collapsed with one kick. "More," said Jason, pointing to the disappearing marbles and the pile of hollow tubes.

"How on earth do I put this thing together?" Lacey muttered, appalled at the part of her brain that refused to kick in whenever it came to fixing or building or mathematics. Rosie was the math person, and Lacey's strong suit was English. "Get a hold of yourself," she said out loud. "It's a toy. We're not talking NASA here." She set about constructing her own rickety structure, with runways leading nowhere. Lacey found a set of measuring cups and placed them beneath the tubing so that the runaway marbles landed with a satisfying plop into the containers instead of whizzing across the living-room floor.

"Books?" said Lacey as Jason punched buttons on a computer robot until a monotonous stream of alphabet letters, simple words, and nursery rhymes jangled her nerves.

"Milky?" Lacey whispered into Jason's ear as he scribbled in crayon on an album cover that he had pulled off the cabinet shelf.

Jason ignored her and chose a blue crayon to obliterate Carly Simon's face.

"No!" said Lacey, pulling the album away. "No no no!"

Jason's eyes filled with tears and his lips trembled into a frown. His cheeks grew flushed as he started to cry. Lacey put her arms around him and patted him and rocked him and tried to distract him with crayons and a coloring book. She walked with the squalling baby into the kitchen. Balancing him on her hip, she took a bottle of milk out of the refrigerator. Karen Drew's directions were all a blur to her now as she tried to recall if she was supposed to heat the bottle. Lacey turned on the faucet marked "hot," but Jason grabbed the bottle and pulled it to his mouth. Cold milk it was, then.

Lacey abandoned the rest of Karen's rules. Forget the *Guys and Dolls* song. No books for Jason, who drank his bottle with half-closed eyes, his chest heaving an occasional sob until at last he fell asleep.

Lacey sighed and placed him gently in his crib, popping the pacifier squarely into his mouth. He sucked contentedly and slept on.

When Karen and Bob Drew returned, the apartment was quiet except for the low droning of the television. Karen tiptoed into the baby's room and touched the top of her son's head. He was alive and well. Bob Drew gave Lacey a twenty-dollar bill, which Lacey pocketed without looking at it, and asked her if she would sit for them every Saturday night.

Lacey said yes.

It had been two years since Lacey had first started watching Jason. At 6:45 on Saturday evening, Tony telephoned, like clockwork, for her weekly Saturday-night advice. Once in a while, she'd beg her friend to ditch her job and come along. "Don't make me go alone tonight," she pleaded. "Call the Drews and tell them you have the flu."

"You know I can't," said Lacey, laughing. "Take Caroline with you to Sal's party. If there's nobody there that you like, the two of you can always bowl."

Tony was not convinced. "My butt jiggles when I bowl," she complained.

"Caroline has no butt at all," said Lacey. "Would you like that better? Besides, my mother says that you remind her of Marilyn Monroe, except for the hair. Jell-O on springs."

"Did somebody call my name?" said Leonora, sailing into the room.

"Ma, didn't you compare Tony to Marilyn Monroe?" Lacey held the receiver toward her mother.

"You're a beautiful girl," Leonora yelled into the air.

"I told you," said Lacey.

"She had a fat stage and a thin stage," whined Tony. "Ask your mother which one."

Lacey groaned. "My mother will say you should be thankful for the comparison."

"Your mother says get ready for babysitting," quipped Leonora.

"Gotta go make some money, Marilyn," said Lacey, hanging up.

Lacey threw some books in her knapsack and addressed her mother. "Tony wants me to go to a party with her. But I tell you, Ma, Jason is so easy now that I hate to give up the money."

"So don't," said Leonora, bending to massage the back of her left calf.

"You wouldn't believe how much better he is with me than he is with his mother," Lacey said smugly. "He has tantrums with his parents, but hardly ever pulls that stuff when I'm around."

"Welcome to the real world," said Leonora. "Children take it out on their parents. They're not afraid to show us their worst side." Leonora ran a finger down her leg and sighed. "I'm getting varicose veins, like Grandma Pearl," she said. "Vinnie is going to take one look at me in this skirt and run out the door. Why on earth did I say I'd go out with him?"

"Because he asked, Ma," said Lacey.

"What am I, Mount Everest?" said her mother.

"Ma, he's not climbing you, he's taking you out for dinner. I think it's good that you finally said yes."

Leonora put a hand over her heart and patted it rapidly. "He's very good-looking, isn't he, Lacey? And those muscles . . . My heart is racing."

Lacey was appalled. Racing to do what? "Ma!"

"Daddy never had any real muscles. It's nice, for a change."

Nice? thought Lacey. What did her mother plan on doing with her new muscle-bound friend? She refused to contemplate it.

"Maybe I shouldn't be talking to you like this," said Leonora. Maybe you shouldn't, Lacey thought.

"Maybe it's a mistake." Lenora swung open the closet door and held herself erect in front of it. "Not bad," she murmured, "except for the battle scars."

Lacey watched curiously as Leonora squinted at the reflection of her left leg. "These varicose veins are disgusting," she said.

Lacey took pity on her. "Grandma's varicose veins are like spiderwebs, Ma. You just have a sprinkling."

"Oh, that's wonderful," said Leonora, slamming the closet door shut. "Fix the pillows behind your head, Lacey. Plump them."

"You look fine," said Lacey, beating the cushions against the back of the couch with such force that she surprised herself. "Jesus, Mom," she blurted out. "You're making me feel like I'm your mother."

"Oh, Lacey," said Leonora, her face falling. "I'm sorry."

Lacey cocked her head sideways and looked at her, the crinkly eyes, the spray of white hair that cried out for Miss Clairol, the small rounded stomach. "It's not your fault, Ma. It's the twenty-first century. The age of divorce." She appraised her mother's too-short skirt and said guiltily, "You've got great legs, Ma."

"Is that what it is?" said her mother, distracted already. "The age of divorce?" She smiled weakly at her daughter. "You've got my legs, sweetie. We've got Barbara Walters legs. Did you ever notice what great legs Barbara Walters has?" She straightened up the magazines in the rack beside the fireplace. "Lacey!" she said, alarmed. "What if he expects me to light a fire? This fireplace hasn't been cleaned since . . ." Leonora's voice faded. "The house is such a mess. He's going to think we're total slobs."

"Why are you so nervous, Mother?" Lacey said. "It's just dinner. You know, chew the food, swallow, talk. That's what you said to me when I went out to the diner with Charles Pincer."

"That was a mistake, Lacey. If I'd known that he'd just

gotten his license, I would never have let you get in the car with him."

"And you would have mortified me, Mother," said Lacey, an unwelcome vision of Charles and his puffy wet lips coming to mind. She never should have said she would go to the movies with him in the first place. Tony had warned her against it.

"Why even bother with somebody you don't like?" she had scolded.

"For practice?" Lacey had replied.

"Use a pillow."

Tony's wisdom hadn't stopped her, and when Lacey first saw Charles Pincer's face peering out of the family station wagon at her, her heart made a downward swoop. It was a tiny arc of death. Not a buzz or a tingle or a tickle of anything approaching anticipation went through her body. Lacey circled behind the car as she saw Charles lean over and unlock the door on the passenger side. He never got out. Lacey sat down and breathed in the overwhelming smell of a sausage, pepper, and onion hero that was resting half eaten on the dashboard. A can of cream soda was next to the stickshift.

Charles had taken her hand in the movies, massaging her palm with his thumb in a languorous circular motion for so long that it made her skin begin to chafe. She pulled her hand away and scratched her nose as if the itch made it impossible for her ever to hold his hand again. Then as surreptitiously as possible she sniffed the tender area of her palm. She thought it smelled faintly of sausage, peppers, and onions.

After the movie, they'd gone back to the car and

Charles had put the key in the ignition but never bothered to start the engine. He continued his massage on her shoulder this time, turning toward her and gently breathing in her face. The odor of onions tickled her nostrils, not a pleasant smell, and as if her expression revealed her revulsion, he'd removed his hand from around her neck and taken a swig of cream soda. Then he planted a wet kiss on her lips that engorged her senses with the culinary wonders of sausage, onion, peppers, and cream soda. Lacey felt like puking.

As she watched her mother pull in her stomach and smile into the mirror, Lacey remembered how easy it had been to tell Charles that she just wasn't interested. Tony reminded her that it was a cinch if you didn't give a damn. What did you have to lose? After the kiss, Lacey had pulled a tissue out of the tissue box in the compartment next to the can of soda, wiped her mouth, and told Charles that she hoped they could be friends. Charles didn't answer. He simply turned the key in the ignition, screeched out of the parking lot, and took her home. He never asked her out again.

"Vinnie manages a gym," volunteered Leonora as she sucked in her stomach for the twentieth time. "Did you notice that his biceps are even bigger than Joseph's? He's always working out. You should see the mega-vitamin shakes he drinks every day. Extra-large, he orders. I wonder where he wants to go for dinner."

"You can bet it's not going to be McDonald's," said Lacey, flicking aside the living-room curtain to watch for the Drew sedan.

Leonora made a whisper of a sigh. "He sees thousands

64

of beautiful women in leotards every day," she said softly.

"They don't wear leotards anymore, Ma. It's called workout gear." Lacey's sigh was louder. Leonora's fears were beginning to get on her nerves. After all, Lacey was the teenager. Her forty-something mother was not supposed to be going out on a date. She was.

"Oh, I know just what they wear!" Leonora piped up. "They wear those thongs up their behinds that look like dental floss. I don't know how they can exercise in something like that. Shorts and a T-shirt have always worked for me."

Lacey raised an eyebrow. "Maybe he's too high-maintenance for you, Ma. Maybe someone like Mr. Livingstone would be better. He thinks you're beautiful already."

"Vinnie is more my age, honey. He's . . . thirty-something."

Lacey couldn't resist. "What's with the girl who's always standing around with him by the juice bar? Is she the competition?"

Leonora shook her head. "That's Denise. She's an aerobics instructor and a personal trainer. I mentioned something to Vinnie about her. Do you know what he tells me? He says she's too butch for him, can you imagine? He likes more feminine women." She left the room and returned lugging the family's twenty-year-old vacuum cleaner behind her.

Lacey eyed her mother as she bent over the carpet, vacuuming up invisible bits of dust. Was Leonora the feminine type? She supposed so, with her heart-shaped butt that was the bane of Lacey's existence because she had the same pear-shaped figure. As Leonora moved rhythmically back and forth, pushing the metal rod beneath the couch and behind the potted plant, there was nothing masculine about her. "So how come you've never introduced me to Vinnie?" Lacey shouted above the noise.

"Just let me put away this piece of junk," Leonora told Lacey, heading back to the kitchen.

"It's an antique," Lacey called after her. "You can leave it to me in your will."

"I wish we could afford a new one," said Leonora, returning. She undid the top button of her shirt, asking, "Open or closed?"

"Open. It shows off your necklace and you look too prim the other way."

"I am prim. This is the first date I've had since Daddy."

Lacey rose to the sound of honking coming from outside. "Bye, Ma," she called, running for the doorway. "Hope it goes better than my date with Charles Pincer."

"From your mouth to God's ears," said her mother, laughing. "Lacey!"

Lacey stopped short. "What, Ma?"

"Do you want to know the real reason I didn't introduce you to him?"

"Why, Ma?"

"Because if he met you, he'd know what an old fart of a mother he was dating."

Lacey smiled widely. "He'll find out soon enough, Ma," she tossed over her shoulder, closing the door to the sounds of her mother's laughter.

5

♥

Lacey had just settled Jason into bed when she heard the click of the key turning in the door. Bob and Karen Drew marched noisily into the apartment as if they wanted to warn Lacey to stop any unlawful doings. Lacey jumped hastily to her feet, vaguely aware that she had done nothing wrong, but feeling guilty just the same.

"We're home early," Karen Drew said stiffly without a word of explanation. Her face had lost the usual healthy glow of someone who read food labels and ate plenty of fruits and vegetables. Strained and pale-looking, she avoided meeting Lacey's eyes and bent instead to pick up Lacey's knapsack. "What on earth is in here?" she asked, admonishingly, handing it to Lacey with a sagging of the wrist, as if the bag contained a ton of rocks. With a shudder of recognition, Lacey realized that Karen Drew had the shellshocked face of Leonora a few years back. She was mad about something—no, she was furious. Lacey hooked her arms through the straps of her knapsack, pocketed the twenty-dollar bill that Mrs. Drew handed her, murmured a quick goodbye, and followed Bob Drew out the door. Fleeing was the order of the day.

Bob Drew unlocked the car door for her, mumbling to himself, "Don't ever get married." With a slam of the door for emphasis, he said lightly, "Women! You can't live with them and you can't shoot 'em."

Lacey suspected that she was supposed to laugh. She stayed quiet. Bob Drew's joke brought to mind her father during the final few months of the Levine marriage. His tone was innocent but his comedy was lethal. If Leonora forgot to pick up the dry-cleaning, or there were no more envelopes in his home office, Michael Levine would call his wife "Lucy," except that Lucille Ball had smiled such winning smiles in the television series, and Leonora hardly smiled at all anymore. He threatened to use a meatball for softball practice, commenting on its perfect heft, then glancing at his daughters to see if they appreciated his playfulness. If Lacey smiled, however weakly, she was betraying her mother. Her father's grin looked more like a sneer turned upside down, and Bob Drew's expression was uncannily similar.

Post-divorce Leonora would have given him a piece of her mind—she had developed a keen nose for male hostility. But Leonora was a different person around Vinnie Rizzo. Watching her at Herrick's was a revelation to Lacey—her face was lively one moment and coy the next. She didn't titter, but she hung on Vinnie Rizzo's every word, even while making a health shake for another customer. Leonora around Vinnie was sixteen years old. But she still would have told Bob Drew where to go, in no uncertain terms.

Bob Drew started up the car and leaned across Lacey's lap so suddenly that she found herself shielding her chest with her hands. "Seat belt," he said, his mouth close to her ear. Lacey felt her face redden. She caught a whiff of beery breath when he clicked her seat belt into place, which brought the equally abhorrent smell of Charles Pincer to mind. Fermented hops and Bob Drew. Pepper and onions and Charles Pincer. Men in cars with bad breath, the story of her life.

Bob Drew began to talk, steering the car through residential streets. As they pulled into the Levine driveway, Lacey cursed herself for not having her house keys ready. Her employer's one-sided conversation continued as she plunged a hand into her overstuffed knapsack, foraging through a jumble of makeup, pencils, notebooks, half rolls of old Life Savers, and rumpled paperbacks for the keys. Every week for two years, Bob Drew had asked her if she had found a boyfriend yet. This week was no exception. And every week he simply couldn't understand why someone hadn't snapped up a pretty girl like Lacey. Something about the way he said "snapped up" irked her, as if she were a forlorn flower eager to be plucked from its stem by some virile quarterback hurtling across the playing field. He found her, he plucked her, he had her in his hands. Touchdown!

Bob Drew switched off the ignition. "I have a cousin,"

he said, "a freshman in college. I'm going to tell him about you. You're just his type."

Lacey chewed on a knuckle to stop herself from answering, "Having a boyfriend wouldn't make me a complete person, you asshole," or something like that. It would have been an extremely satisfying response, something Leonora might have said. Instead, she heard herself saying, "I don't think my mother would like it if I went out with a college boy."

"Didn't I see her with some pumped-up guy at the health-food store the other day?" Bob Drew's smile was deadly.

"That's Vinnie, a friend of hers," said Lacey, breathing a sigh of relief as her hand touched metal and she pulled out her keys.

"A friend, huh?" said Bob knowingly. "Your sister, Rosie, has a friend she's cozy with, too, doesn't she? You'd better get busy, young lady." He wagged a finger at her.

Rosie. Cozy. Nosy son of a bitch. Lacey let herself out of the car with a grim little goodbye.

"Same time, same place," Bob Drew called back.

Be there or be square, asshole. Sometimes Lacey wondered where her anger sprang from. Lightning struck, and she was a raging fire. One moment she'd be rolling along, happy as a clam because David Potter had smiled at her. Then someone like Kenny would make a comment like "How's it going, Pocahontas?" just because she was wearing some Indian beads, and Lacey would feel such an overwhelming stab of pure hatred that it left her trembling.

Once she told Tony that their art teacher Mr. Harmon annoyed her. "He has the nerve to tell me that my artwork is sloppy," Lacey complained to her friend. "Matisse left his drips in, and they became a part of his painting. Why can't I? Harmon sucks."

Tony, never at a loss for a theory, put down her paintbrush and said, "I think you're mad at all men, Lacey, ever since your father left you."

"Who died and made you God?" Lacey shot back at her. Nostrils flaring, she continued painting the sky a shocking shade of pink. Finally she said, "He didn't leave me, he left my mother. You make it sound like he abandoned me on a doorstep or something."

"If you say so." Tony shrugged. "It just seems like you have this thing about men . . ." She paused, choosing her words carefully. "You think they're the enemy," she said.

"I don't feel that way," Lacey complained. Her voice dropped to a whisper. "If I hated all men, why would I have such a crush on David? Tell me that, smarty-pants."

Tony smiled benevolently. "Don't get me wrong, Lacey. I don't think you're a lesbian. Really I don't."

"Tony"—Lacey spoke between gritted teeth—"I just have a thing about men who are jerks. Period."

"If you say so," said Tony.

As Lacey ran up the walkway to the darkened house, she couldn't help noticing its drooping shutters and shabby appearance. When her mother and father were on speaking terms again, her father had warned Leonora not to put paint on top of stone. Lacey knew by the tilted angle of her mother's chin that paint on stone would be forthcoming. That very weekend Leonora had rigged up a ladder, donned a baggy jumpsuit and a baseball cap, and started painting the house a pure white. Now the paint was chipping, and Lacey thought how nice it would be if Joseph Panteleone had a family member in the contracting business. After all, the Levine mansion's renovation was a far better cause than the clothes on Rosie Levine's back.

Sherman met her at the door with a clipped squeak of a meow. Lacey switched on the hall light and kicked off her shoes so that they flew against the stairwell. She padded into the kitchen and opened the refrigerator. Giving its contents a mindless stare, she froze. A low moaning sound filtered through the back wall up from the cellar. This was definitely not the sound of a house settling. Sherman uttered a second clipped meow and raised her head. Lacey cocked her own head to the side, as if the very movement would sharpen her hearing. The noise continued, shifting in volume and length, like snatches of music from a radio gone bad.

Lacey gripped a large bottle of seltzer, the most immediate weapon at hand. Carefully closing the refrigerator, she slid soundlessly in her socks toward the cellar door. She turned the doorknob slowly, millimeter by millimeter, so that there would be no click of metal. Her feet found each step in the darkness until she had reached the cold cement floor of the basement. As Lacey turned the corner, she saw a brilliant beam of light. Her eyes followed it to its source. Her jaw dropped at what she saw, and she whispered out loud, "What are you doing?"

Two interlocking bodies sprang apart, blinding Lacey with flashes of skin so that she forced herself to look away. Two bodies scrambled for cover, cot creaking, clothing flapping, zippers sliding up, the click of snaps, the smallest grunt of effort, a swinging of hair, a tissue wiping a chin.

Rosie spoke first. "Why are you home so early?" she said hoarsely.

Lacey stared, wide-eyed, clutching the bottle of seltzer to her chest. "They didn't stay out as long as usual," she said mechanically. "They went to the movies."

"Gotta go." Two words from Joseph, who bounded past her and took the stairs three at a time. "Call you." Another pair of words shot over his shoulder.

"I'm going to bed," Rosie said coolly.

Lacey turned to watch her, heard a brush of denim as her sister rounded the corner. She didn't move a muscle. "Are you coming?" she heard Rosie say.

Lacey picked up the flashlight and circled the basement with it. This was foreign territory to her now, and she was a space traveler on alien ground. The washing machine, the dryer, the barrels, the clothesline, strange interlopers in the glimmer of light. She beamed the flashlight across the length of the cot, illuminating the zigzag design of the mattress, a small tear in the fabric, a stain. She felt a clutch in her stomach as she remembered the wet spot.

"Sherman?" she cried, circulating the light again. The cat was nowhere to be found. She switched off the flashlight and set it upright on the basement floor. Turning her back on the cot and its mattress, which drooped in the middle, she dragged her feet up the steps to the kitchen. Rosie stood waiting, arms folded.

Her sister sounded less certain now. "Are you going to tell Ma?" she said.

Lacey put the seltzer bottle carefully on the kitchen table and swung open the freezer door, glad for the rush of cold air on her cheeks. "I guess not," she mumbled into the cartons of veggie burgers and frozen yogurt. When she turned around, Rosie was gone.

Leonora came home well after midnight and was humming as she mounted the stairs. Lacey heard water running in the bathroom, the scrubbing of teeth, the click of the hall light switch. She quickly assumed a sleeping position, spreading her hair out on the pillow, placing an arm slightly askew. Her bedroom door opened slowly.

"Lacey?" Leonora said hopefully. Eyes closed, Lacey held her breath. She could smell the sweet scent of her mother's favorite perfume. Vinnie must have smelled it, just as Joseph must have sniffed her sister's scent downstairs in the basement. Leonora stood there for a moment, then closed the door quietly. "Rosie?" Lacey heard her call, down the hall, outside her sister's bedroom door. No one answered.

Lacey cradled her head in her arms under a mound of quilting. She pressed her nose against her skin, and breathed in. No scent. Colorless. Odorless. Blank.

Leonora was chatty at breakfast. She read snatches of an article from behind the Sunday paper, lowering its pages periodically to address one daughter or the other.

"The restaurant was called La Bacca," she said. "The maître d' knew Vinnie."

"He takes all his girls there," said Rosie, pushing aside her plate of scrambled eggs.

Leonora was unfazed. "He's a bachelor. He eats out a lot. So what? The food was"—she held up three fingers and kissed them with a flourish—"*magnifico!*" Leonora surveyed her daughter's blank faces. "Full of life, aren't you?" she said. "So, Lacey. How was babysitting?"

Lacey glanced over at her sister. "I think Mr. and Mrs. Drew had a fight. They came home early, so I was back by ten."

"How did you know they had a fight?" Leonora asked.

"I'm an expert at it."

Her mother nodded. "I suppose you are," she said. "And you, my dear Rosie," she addressed her daughter brightly, artificially. "How's Joseph?"

"He's fine," said Rosie, pushing away from the table, but not before Lacey caught sight of the flush in her sister's cheeks. "We might see each other later," she said quickly. "I'm going to do a load of laundry."

Lacey washed dishes while her mother dried. Her eyes followed her sister as she carried a basket of soiled clothes down the steps. Rosie's arms hugged the plastic, her hips undulating back and forth as she descended the staircase. In her mind Lacey saw the flash of limbs and movement. She realized with a start that Rosie was a stranger to her now, a creature whose round cheeks and tousled gold hair no longer spelled primness and prettiness, smartness and conventionality as she'd thought. They spelled sex.

6

♥

Grandma Pearl appeared on the scene shortly after Rosie had completed the wash cycle but before Lacey had totally lost her mind listening to her mother talk about the charms of Vinnie Rizzo.

Leonora put down her coffee cup and darted across the floor. "Darling Ma," she said happily, throwing her arms around her mother.

Grandma took her daughter's hands, leaned back, and appraised her.

"What?" said Leonora, casting her eyes bashfully at her feet. "What are you looking at?"

Grandma's eyes were a clear, alert green surrounded by a fine web of wrinkles that she blamed on smoking. They took in everything. "Someone's downright perky today," she said.

"I haven't been perky in twenty years, Ma," said Leonora, the color rising in her cheeks.

"Then you must be eating your Wheaties," Grandma said with a twinkle in her eye.

Leonora flashed her a smile so big her gums showed. "Raisin bran, Ma. I prefer raisin bran," she said.

"She's the blushing bride, isn't she, Grandma?" Lacey said. She wondered if Grandma could detect the sarcasm in her voice.

"It's nice to see her happy," said Grandma, raising one dark eyebrow ever so slightly.

Lacey was relieved by her grandmother's presence. Relieved from having to act as a sounding board for her mother's trials and tribulations. "You're going to stay for a while, aren't you, Grandma?" she said hopefully. "I was just leaving to meet Tony at the deli."

"Be back in time to have supper with Grandma and me," said Leonora. "Maybe she can make us some stuffed cabbage without the meat. Do you think you can do that, Ma?"

"Not only can I do that, but I can stuff it with bits of that vegetarian burger you like so much. How about that?"

Lacey grabbed her denim jacket and slipped out of the house. There was an edge of winter to the air as she sucked in cold breaths. She hesitated at the corner and made the decision to take the long way around to the deli. Perhaps the exercise would clear her head. It astonished her, the switch from drama in the basement one night to vegetarian stuffed cabbage the next. Her brain had taken a Polaroid snapshot of Rosie and Joseph, all limbs and motion, which kept springing into view against her will. What would her mother say if she knew? What if Leonora's date with Vinnie had gone terribly wrong, and her mother had interrupted the business in the basement? Lacey wished with all her heart that she had. Let her mother catch sight of her well-behaved child, writhing and grappling with Joseph Panteleone. Let Leonora feel the betrayal of Rosie the paramour instead of Rosie the bookworm.

Lacey sighed. And what a betrayal. When Rosie was born and Michael Levine had crowned her "Rose," the nurses had dubbed her "Miss Rosie." The best baby in the nursery, she rarely cried, and wore a constant beatific smile on her face. It was all family history, the kind that Leonora bored relatives with at holiday dinners, how Rosie had been their little princess, sedate at birth. No one would ever have dared to label Rosie an "I Love Lucy" type. She was practical, not reckless; punctual, not wacky. She did her laundry without being reminded, she got straight A's on her report cards, sewed her own hems, never forgot choir practice in the morning, and sang like an angel. Except that Rosie, the angel, the good girl, was no longer Miss Rosie. The business in the basement had finished all that.

Lacey plucked a few leaves from a nearby privet. Grandma Pearl had taken one look at Leonora and had known that something was different. Leonora had taken one look at Rosie that morning and had asked her to pass the butter. Starry-eyed and totally oblivious Leonora. Was her mother so steeped in Vinnie Rizzo that she couldn't see the forest for the trees? Vinnie and Leonora, limbs interlocking. Perish the thought. Perhaps Grandma's antennae were more finely tuned than Leonora's. Could Grandma Pearl detect the subtle changes in Rosie? Could Grandma Pearl detect the sex?

Lacey snapped the leaves together between her fingers. She suspected what her mother would say if she found out. Prior to Vinnie Rizzo's appearance, Leonora had been sensible, like Rosie, claiming, "Rosie and I use our heads, and Daddy and Lacey follow their hearts." Neither girl liked hearing it, but it was the truth. In Lacey's mind, the truth had backfired on Leonora. When the fighting had erupted, Lacey had gathered up courage and pressed her ear to the bedroom wall. She'd heard her father plead, "I fell in love, Lee. I never planned on it. I never wanted to hurt you or the girls, ever ever ever. It just happened." Leonora had snarled at him, "What do you want me to do, Michael? Buy a T-shirt that says 'Shit happens' and forget about it? You've ruined our lives!" Lacey couldn't possibly remind her mother, "You always told us, Ma, that Daddy followed his heart."

Lacey threw the fistful of leaves on the pavement. No, after the initial shock of it all, and the ranting and raving, Leonora would most likely inquire, "Are you using protection, Rosie?"

Lacey felt her stomach dip. It hadn't occurred to her before that Rosie was putting something other than Lacey's image of her in jeopardy. If she didn't take it upon herself to tell Leonora, then who was going to make sure that her sister was taking care of herself in the big bad world where she could catch some awful disease or get pregnant? Nobody.

Lacey picked up speed as a veritable slide show of AIDS-afflicted patients dying in hospitals fast-forwarded through her head. Blind, sunken-eyed, hollow-cheeked, skeletal, unable to eat, spot-ridden. A funeral, with Leonora and Grandma and Lacey sobbing over the casket. An empty bedroom with a closet full of preppy clothes that would never be worn again. Lacey slowed down a little. Perhaps Rosie had thought about birth control. Could she possibly have consulted Dr. Locker, their mother's gynecologist, who had examined each of them for the first time last year? Lacey pictured his mournful face, his crop of wiry white hair, and shook her head. She couldn't imagine Rosie asking him for help. Did muscle-bound Joey carry protection with him? Could muscle-bound Joey even put on a condom? Lacey recalled the story about the boys' gym teacher using a cucumber to demonstrate the proper way to use a condom. Lacey nearly snickered out loud—Joseph Panteleone could barely change a lightbulb, which was the reason he was working the cash register at his father's place instead of apprenticing to be a plumber with his uncle. Rumor had it that he had flunked the condom test, big-time.

Lacey passed the flower shop with its miniature pond. Perched in front of it was a loony-looking scarecrow, a black crow dangling comically from his sleeve. She couldn't help smiling as she recalled Tony's gleeful face the day she'd run into the art room and told Caroline and Lacey about Kenny Lerner's lunchtime discovery. He had come across the gym teacher's brown paper bag on a tray in the cafeteria. Mr. Muni's name was written across it in felt-tip pen. Kenny had sneaked a peek inside the bag and found a list of boys' names, some crossed off, some circled, along with a long cucumber and a condom. Kenny had spread the word that the circled names, Charles Pincer and Joseph Panteleone among them, had failed the condom test. In hygiene class, they were simply unable to slide the condom onto the cucumber without tearing the latex.

That was before Lacey had ever thought about Rosie and Joseph "doing the dirty," so she had joked to Rosie later that afternoon, "Is it true that Joseph flunked the cucumber test in Mr. Muni's class?"

Rosie had been incensed. "What are you, out of your mind?" she fumed. "Joseph's told me all about hygiene class. Mr. Muni showed them all how to put the bag on the cucumber, once, in front of the class. What do you think, every one of the boys went up in front of the room and tried it? That's the most ridiculous thing I've ever heard." Then she'd stalked out of the room.

Lacey started watching Rosie and Joseph after that. But they rarely touched, and they never kissed in front of anybody. Once in a while, they held hands. Lacey came to the conclusion that Joseph and Rosie weren't "doing it" at all. When she told Tony her theory, Tony said, "She used the word 'bag' for condom? That's a bit suspect, don't you think? It's a guy word." But Lacey hadn't thought it meant a thing.

Lacey sucked in some more cold air as the horrible thought occurred to her that Joseph Panteleone and Charles Pincer might not have been singled out because they had failed the cucumber test. What if they were the boys who had confessed to having had intercourse? Lacey gagged at the thought of anyone having sex with sausage, pepper, and onion Charles. She couldn't help conjuring the vision of Charles Pincer fitting a condom over a large piece of Italian sausage. Lacey snorted. Tony would have suggested a cocktail weenie instead.

Lacey shook her head. The real problem was Rosie. She blushed at her own colossal naïveté. Just because she had never seen Joey and Rosie kissing in public didn't mean that they were chaste in private. Lacey took the palm of her hand and hit it against her forehead like a person in a cartoon. How could she be so stupid? She caught sight of Tony sitting cross-legged on the cement sidewalk in front of Jake's. Her spirits lifted a little. Tony toasted her with a can of soda and pushed herself up from the pavement, just as Caroline popped out from behind the pillar and waved.

"Oh, my aching bones," said Tony, brushing off her bottom.

"Oh, your aching butt." Scott McGraw slid next to her. Lacey could tell by Tony's grin that she was pleased by his remark even though it referred to her posterior. She drew a quick breath as David Potter appeared. He was dressed like Scott, in layers of T-shirt and denim, except that Scott was wearing soft blue baggy jeans that threatened to slide down past his rear end to his knees and David had on his weird green pants. As Lacey met him face to face, she noted that his pimple was gone. Her heart did its usual hyped-up dance, but she had other matters on her mind. Today she needed to talk to Tony.

"I have to tell you something," she said urgently, casting a glance at Caroline.

Caroline took no notice. She said to David in a voice that was low and syrupy, "I like your green pants. They're really cool." She pushed back a hank of blond hair that fell into her saucer-round blue crystal eyes. One eye started twitching.

David didn't seem to notice. "Thanks," he said, putting a hand out to finger the choker around Caroline's neck. "I like your necklace."

Lacey's eyes met Tony's. Her friend's eyebrows were raised. "Is it true blondes have more fun?" Tony mumbled under her breath.

Scott McGraw ran a hand through his blond hair. "I always thought so," he joked.

David yanked the deli door open, clipping Lacey on her side. He turned. "Coffee?" he asked without an apology.

Tony gave Lacey a look that said, "And you like this insufferable person?"

"I'll just get a soda," said Lacey, following behind David so closely that she trod on the back of his sneaker. Never mind, she thought, at least she'd left Caroline behind.

"Watch the Nikes," David said as he rapped on the counter surface.

"Dave, Lacey, what can I do you for?" Rob was stacking paper coffee cups behind the counter. "I've convinced Jake to get rid of the Styrofoam and go for paper," he said. "Cool, huh?"

"My environmentalist," gushed Lacey, immediately embarrassed by her response. Why was it so much easier to flirt with Rob than David? Because it didn't matter?

Rob appeared to enjoy it. He took a deep bow and said, "At your service, my pretty."

"You two are wackos," said David, ordering a coffee.

"I'll have an orange juice," said Lacey.

"Aghhh," said David, making a face. "How can you drink that stuff?"

"Notice her teeth, hair, and eyes, David my boy? That beauty is all from vitamin C, isn't it, Lacey?" Rob winked at her.

"David only likes vitamin E, don't you, Dave?" said Lacey, winking back. "It's good for the sex drive." Her heart started hammering at the boldness of her remark.

Rob whistled, and David looked at her, startled. "Is it?" he said.

"My mother works at Herrick's, so I ought to know." Lacey tossed off the words, trying to cover her embarrassment. Good heavens, she thought, is it vitamin E or D?

David snorted. "You ought to know, huh, Lacey?" He rolled his eyes for extra measure. "You and your sister. Why do you think Joey P. is always pumping iron? He's not getting any!"

"Maybe he just likes working out," said Rob, holding out a coffee and an orange juice. "Drink up," he said. "Don't let it stunt your growth, David."

David grunted and walked out the door.

"What's eating him?" said Rob.

Lacey sipped on her orange juice. A feeling of cold despair crept into her brain and settled down for the winter. Why couldn't she have a crush on Rob instead of on David? David was either insulting her or walking out the door, or both in rapid succession.

"Guess I'll go outside," she said feebly.

Rob started stacking paper coffee cups so high that they threatened to topple over. "Maybe we can get together sometime," he said.

"They're going to fall," said Lacey, desperate for an answer as she pointed to the tower of cups instead.

"Oh, right," said Rob, dividing the stack in two just as Tony burst through the door.

"Tell," said Tony. Rob receded like wallpaper.

"Outside," said Lacey, waving goodbye as Tony crooked an arm through hers and dragged her out the door.

Despite the fact that Scott McGraw was hanging around the doorway, Tony agreed to huddle under the alcove with Lacey.

"So?"

Lacey took a deep breath. "I found out what the noises in the basement were," she said.

"What?"

Lacey peered to the right and left of her. No one seemed to take any notice of them. "Rosie and Joseph were doing it."

"No!" said Tony, wide-eyed. She hesitated. "Do you mean . . . *doing* it? Or making out."

"I walked in on them buck-naked," said Lacey, pulling back to see the effect of her remark on Tony.

"The slut!" Tony blurted out.

Lacey felt herself reeling. She couldn't tell if Tony was joking or not, and even though she was horribly shocked by the discovery, the remark made Lacey's stomach turn.

Tony tried to make amends. "You mean, Little Miss Perfect actually surprised us all?"

Lacey couldn't help defending her sister. "They've been going together for ages, Tony."

"Pressure," said Tony, nodding wisely.

"Do you think so?" said Lacey.

"I know so. That's what happens after a while."

"So what do I do about it? Do I tell my mother?"

"Why would you tell your mother? Rosie would kill you."

Lacey nodded miserably.

"She's a big girl, you know, in more ways than one. She can handle herself." Tony's eyes slid toward Scott. "Did you hear what he said back there?" she whispered.

"Something about your butt," Lacey said dispiritedly. She didn't even have the heart to tell her about Rob. He was nice and all that, and Lacey was flattered, but it was David who really counted. And worrying about Rosie was already getting in the way.

Grandma's vegetarian stuffed cabbage wasn't half bad, but still Leonora ate it sparingly, and Rosie pushed the pale greenish ball from one side of her plate to the other.

"What's the matter, you don't like it?" said Grandma between bites.

"I'm just not that hungry," said Rosie, smiling apologetically at Grandma.

"Me neither," said Leonora.

"I like it," said Lacey, washing down a mouthful with a swig of milk.

"What's your excuse?" Grandma said, eyeing Leonora. "You asked me to make it for you."

"She's in love," Lacey said bitterly.

Rosie looked surprised. "She is?"

Grandma's eyes sparkled. "He already called her this afternoon to ask her out for next Saturday. That's eager!"

"He's competing," said Leonora. "A bodybuilding contest. I'm going to watch him, and then we'll have a late dinner. You girls can fend for yourselves, can't you?"

"Don't we always?" Lacey said so sharply that Leonora's head jerked.

"Lacey!" Grandma's voice was steely. "Don't be sarcastic. Your mother deserves some time for herself. Do you want me to come and give you girls supper?"

"No." Lacey knew how nasty she sounded, but she didn't care.

Rosie's "no" had been a quick second. "Joseph and I are going to grab a movie," she said. "He wants to see the new Sylvester Stallone flick."

"Don't go running around so much, Rosie. You're looking downright peaked. And you eat like a bird."

"Joey likes me to be thin," said Rosie.

Lacey saw her mother cringe. "Tell Joey to go out with a toothpick if he feels that way," Leonora protested. "What is he, a moron?"

"Maaaa," Rosie whined. "I like being thin, too."

"Don't get too thin," Leonora warned. "You look lovely the way you are."

Lacey chewed on a piece of Italian bread and snickered. Rosie liked being thin for Joseph. For once, her mother was being a mother again. Lacey made up her mind that Rosie was the moron, not Joseph. Joseph was getting his workout in more places than the Glenwood Health Club. He was getting plenty of it in the Levine basement.

Slathering another piece of bread with some butter, Lacey barely had time to sink her teeth into it before she heard her mother say, "Haven't you had enough, Lacey?"

She looked hard at her mother, then at her sister, who was listlessly tunneling with her fork through a piece of stuffed cabbage. Lacey wished with all her heart that she could zap what she was thinking into her mother's brain: Rosie is getting more than thin, Ma. Open up your goddamned eyes and see what Rosie is getting. Are you so blinded by hope and Vinnie Rizzo that you can't see anything else? Look at me, for a change, Ma. How about looking at me?

"Lacey, I said haven't you had enough?" her mother repeated.

"I have, Mother," Lacey answered, throwing the bread down on the table. "I really have."

7

♥

When Karen Drew telephoned to tell Lacey that she wouldn't be needing her the following Saturday night, Lacey was hardly surprised. In Lacey's eyes, the couple's behavior the week before had all the earmarks of a bang-up fight, and she had already begun using her imagination. Had Bob Drew met someone younger and prettier, someone without the sagging childbirth belly that Karen Drew and her mother so often complained about? Leonora had once complimented Lacey on her smooth stomach. "I remember the days before stretch marks," she'd said wistfully. Perhaps Bob Drew had found a meat-eating bimbo, minus the stretch marks.

"You could be dead wrong," said Tony as they walked home from school together on Monday afternoon. "Just because they had a fight doesn't mean he's run off and left her. They could have kissed and made up by now. Maybe they've gone upstate to watch the leaves change or something."

"I don't think so," said Lacey. "Something's brewing. Remember how you used to babysit for your neighbors on Wednesday nights?"

"Sure. They went to a marriage counselor every week. Then they told me they wouldn't need me anymore, but I still hear them screaming their heads off next door." Tony paused to remove the rubber band from her ponytail and shook her head vigorously. "I have a headache," she complained.

"I like it better down," said Lacey, lifting up a strand of her friend's hair. "Mark my words," she added, shifting the conversation back to the Drews. "I could be babysitting on Wednesday nights sometime in the very near future." Lacey hesitated. "That is, if Mr. Drew will go."

It was Tony's turn to hesitate. "Did your father go to counseling?" she said.

"Nope. My mother said he wouldn't." Lacey repeated the words. "He wouldn't." As clear as day, she could remember Leonora railing at her father to "see a professional," and Michael Levine's response, which filtered so clearly through the bedroom wall. "I don't need to see anyone professional," he'd announced to his wife. "I don't love you anymore."

Lacey felt a familiar sensation in her chest, like a balloon imploding, her own peculiar brand of heart attack. She had felt it then, and she felt it now. No matter how many books on divorce Grandma Pearl had brought home from the library, no matter how many times her father had told her that he loved her, the words continued to chill her. "I don't love you anymore." She had learned about the singular and the plural "you" in elementary school. The "you" of "I don't love you anymore" could be plural, couldn't it? It was the "you" that haunted her.

"What about little Jason?" Tony startled Lacey out of her memory.

Lacey spoke briskly. "Jason will survive. I have."

"But you've changed," said Tony. "You're not the same."

"I'm smarter," said Lacey.

"Maybe," said Tony, stretching the rubber band over her index finger and pulling back on it. "Gotcha!" she shouted as it flew against the mailbox. "What do you think your father would do if he knew about Rosie?"

Lacey tripped over a paving stone and steadied herself against Tony. "Don't even think about it," she said. She felt a pang at the thought that she couldn't tell anyone. "I think my grandmother would be the best person to tell. She wouldn't start ranting and raving like my parents would."

"Duh, Lacey," said Tony. "She'd go straight to your mother. She'd have to."

"I suppose." Lacey sighed deeply.

Tony patted Lacey's shoulder, then brightened. "This means that you can go to Ellen Hopper's Halloween party!"

Lacey was less than thrilled. "I don't have a costume," she said glumly, "and I don't have any money to buy one."

"That's no excuse," said Tony. "You can use my cat

mask and my tail from last year." She lifted up a hank of red hair and let it drop. "I'm going as Raggedy Ann, and I don't even need a wig!" Tony flung an arm around Lacey. "And you, my dear, are bitchy enough to go as a cat."

Leonora spent too much time in the bathroom preparing for her date, bright-eyed and hopeful in black Lycra pants and a short emerald-green shirt that showed just a glimpse of her midriff. It was a *soupçon* too much for Lacey, who stuck her head inside the bathroom and blanched at the sight of it.

"What's with the top?" she said, leaning against the doorjamb and waiting for her mother to notice her cat outfit. Lacey coughed several times, fanning the air with her hands. "Mother, I feel like I'm wearing your perfume just by standing in the same room with you! You'll asphyxiate him!"

"Vinnie likes the way I smell," Leonora said mildly, shifting in front of the mirror as she eyed her midriff for any telltale flab. "Sweetheart!" she said, catching sight of her daughter's reflection. "You look adorable! Turn around."

Lacey made a pirouette as her mother beamed.

"So beautiful," said Leonora, her eyes glistening. "So young." She straightened up her shoulders and turned back to the mirror, her hand hovering over a basket of makeup. Plucking out a compact, she stroked a line of blush along her right cheekbone. "I feel like I'm back in high school," she murmured, dusting the other cheekbone. "Oh God," said Leonora, rubbing at her cheeks with her wrist. "What I need is a face-lift."

"You look fine," said Lacey, gritting her teeth as she watched her mother purse her lips in the mirror. She felt a rage in her chest so powerful that she pressed a hand against her sternum.

When Leonora smiled seductively at her reflection, Lacey exploded. "Stop looking at yourself!" she shouted. "One moment you're crying about how beautiful I am and the next moment you're acting like you're the only one who's ever gone on a date before! You're my mother, you know!"

Leonora turned to look at her daughter. "You're losing an ear," she said softly, reaching a hand out to stick it back on her head.

"Don't," said Lacey, springing back. "I can do it myself."

Leonora framed her face with her hands, pulling back at the skin by her cheeks.

"Don't tell me again that you need a face-lift," Lacey said bitterly. "I don't want to hear it."

"This face is forty-three years old," her mother said quietly, stroking the skin in a circular motion. "I'm never going to get any younger. I'm never going to get any prettier. I've got my face, my brain, and my heart. I want to use them all, honey, before it's too late."

"I need you," said Lacey, brushing away at a tear that trembled at the edge of her eye.

"I know, honey. I know." Leonora put her arms around her daughter, resting her forty-three-year-old cheek

93

against Lacey's. "I'm acting like a damned fool," she whispered into her ear. "I can feel it. I can see it. I can't seem to help it, though."

"Try, Ma," said Lacey, pulling away from her mother. "Try to help it. Because it bothers the hell out of me."

Rosie wandered into the hallway, clutching her stomach. "Don't be so hard on her," she admonished her sister. "Mom deserves a life of her own." Rosie rapped on the wall outside the bathroom even though the door was open. "I need to get in there badly, Ma. I had a hamburger with Joseph that did me in."

"I told you never to eat that garbage," said Leonora, giving herself one more glance in the mirror before exiting. Rosie rushed inside and slammed the bathroom door shut.

Lacey and her mother popped eyes at each other as they were treated to a series of violent retching noises.

"Rosie," her mother said anxiously. "Are you all right?"

"Does it sound like I'm all right?" Rosie's voice was muffled.

Leonora was silent for a few seconds. "Do you want me to stay home?" she said.

"No," said Rosie miserably. "I just hope Joseph doesn't get this."

"I can stay," said Leonora, peering at her watch.

"Or I can," said Lacey, ready to rip off her cat ears in a heartbeat. She held her breath as Rosie retched into the toilet bowl one more time.

"Sweetheart?" said Leonora.

At last, Rosie said, "I'm feeling a little better now."

"Are you sure?" Leonora put her ruby-painted mouth close to the bathroom door.

"I'm sure," whispered Rosie.

Leonora leaned in toward her younger daughter. "Do you think I should stay?" she whispered. "Maybe I should stay home with Rosie."

Lacey breathed in Leonora's fragrance and took pity on her. "Go, Ma," she said. "Rosie says she's feeling better."

Leonora hugged Lacey and rapped on the bathroom door. "I'll call later, honey." Then she bounded down the stairs in black Victorian boots that Lacey suspected were Vinnie's favorites, and left the house.

Ellen Hopper lived north of the railroad tracks, "in the posh part of town," as Leonora put it. The houses were sprawling and spacious there, with property and acreage instead of back yards and front yards. No one on the north side of town weeded, seeded, or mowed his own land. Instead, an army of trucks equipped with mowers and scurrying gardeners lined the streets five days a week.

The Hopper mansion was hung with every imaginable Halloween decoration. No doubt someone had been paid to do that, too. Tiny plastic pumpkins swung from the branches of the dogwood tree, tombstones dotted the front acreage complete with "Rest in Peace" signs. There was a scarecrow sagging in a chair on the front porch, a skeleton dangling from the colonial-style lamppost. Orange plastic garbage bags with pumpkin faces were stuffed with leaves, sitting on the lawn.

When Tony rang the Hopper doorbell, the sound of

hideous screaming filled the porch. Lacey, Caroline, and Tony stared wide-eyed at each other and burst into laughter. A raven-haired witch with matching lips and three-inch fingernails swung open the front door.

"You rang?" she intoned.

"Ellen?" Tony squinted at her. "Is that you?"

"It sure is," said Ellen. "My parents are down the block at a party of their own! We have the house to ourselves!"

The girls crowded around a huge gilt-framed mirror hanging in the alcove. Lacey couldn't help admiring herself in her fetching cat ears and painted whiskers, her nose a pink triangle and her green eyes highlighted by shimmering olive eye shadow. A black furry tail which Rosie had sewn on the back of Lacey's black jumpsuit swung behind her. For once, her mother was right. She did look absolutely adorable.

Tony's hair was in two braids and her nose was blue. A sprinkling of freckles and a gingham dress completed the outfit. She looked cross-eyed at herself in the mirror. "I think I got Raggedy Ann mixed up with Pippi Long-stocking," she said mournfully.

Lacey laughed. "With a little bit of Dorothy from *The Wizard of Oz* thrown in," she said, lowering her voice to a whisper as she caught sight of David Potter. "Who's David supposed to be in the eye patch?" she said, casting her eyes in his direction. "Captain Hook?"

"Where's the hook?" whispered Tony. "And what's with the mini plastic sword?"

David sidled up to them, twirling a tiny cutlass in the air. "Ahoy, maties!" he bellowed.

"Captain Hook?" said Lacey timidly.

"I'm a generic pirate," David replied, running his eyes up and down Lacey's cat outfit. "Meooow, meoooow! Sleek and sassy, little Miss Kitty!" He wiped a hand across his forehead and shook the imaginary sweat off it.

"Oh brother," Tony mumbled under her breath as she squeezed past Lacey. She took hold of her friend's tail and yanked it. "He thinks you're the cat's meow," she murmured. Then she raised her voice to address Caroline, who was dressed as a princess, complete with tiara and wand. "Let's mingle, Cinderella."

David rubbed a shoulder against Lacey. He took his plastic sword and touched the tip of her left cat ear with it. "Do you want a drink?" he said. "Kenny brought a six-pack."

Lacey nodded, watching him with her eyes as he threaded his way through the living room and into the kitchen. She realized too late that she should have followed him. He might never come back.

Lacey surveyed the party. She tried to beat back the familiar feeling that she was the only person who wasn't having the most wonderful time in the world. After all, the boy she had a crush on was getting her a drink. Never mind that she didn't even like beer. Or that wet spots had begun to form under her armpits and her heart was hammering like crazy. She was off to a very good start.

Lacey stood snapping her fingers in time to the music, which was so loud that she could barely recognize the tune. She never could get the hang of snapping, but no one would know the difference with the music blaring.

She hoped that she looked totally at ease, standing there alone in the living room, moving her hips ever so slightly and snapping soundlessly. As long as she didn't look like a wallflower.

The party had acquired a buzz. Some people were dancing furiously, and others were clustered in different parts of the huge living room, laughing and talking. Lacey resisted the urge to stand on tiptoe and crane her neck to look for David. Where was he? Tony would tell her she was crazy. She didn't even like alcohol, and here she was, waiting for a drink she hated as much as coffee. Leonora wouldn't like it any better. Be true to yourself, she had always cautioned her girls. Drinking and drugs were out. So were a bunch of teenagers in a house with no chaperone. Lacey made up her mind to take small sips of the disgusting stuff, and perhaps David wouldn't see her hands trembling. As for the missing chaperone, what her mother didn't know wouldn't hurt her.

Lacey sighed and stood on tiptoe to look for David. Screw waiting, she thought. She parted her way through the throngs in the living room, recognizing only a few faces behind the masks as she threaded past ghosts and mummies, clowns and Draculas and Frankenstein's monsters. Daggers were popular, plunged into bare male chests with lots of surrounding red ooze. A zombie nodded his head at her and Lacey turned away quickly as she recognized Charles Pincer beneath the mask.

Tony waved as she chatted merrily away with Barbara Buttle, a nice girl who didn't seem bothered that her tiny upper frame ballooned terribly into an enormous backside, or even that her name brought to everyone's attention her very worst feature. Mercifully, she was a pumpkin today. Lacey knew that it was not for nothing that Tony and Barbara were back to back with Scott McGraw as he gyrated on the dance floor with Ellen Hopper. Lacey could tell by Tony's eyes that she was faking her own fun. Ellen was batting a witchy hip against Scott McGraw as Tony's eyes grew glittery with jealousy.

By the time Lacey had reached the kitchen, David was nowhere to be found. The table was littered with empty beer cans and bowls with the dust of potato chips. She wet the end of her index finger and pressed it to the bottom of a dish, licking off the salty yellow fragments.

Lacey glanced at the clock. Tony had convinced them to sit at home watching Halloween specials with her until it was fashionably late, and it was already ten-thirty. She pulled her body erect and lifted her chin, the whisker makeup cracking on her face. "I will have fun," she said out loud, forcing herself to smile.

David was not in the dining room, either. Lacey grabbed a handful of candy corn and popped some into her mouth. She savored its sweetness, debating whether to give up the search or not. It would never do to look desperate.

Lacey rounded the corner and found herself heading up the stairs. The carpeting was so plush and thick that she glanced behind her to see if she'd left footprints. Rosie had confessed a while back that she had been embarrassed to bring Joseph home with her because of their threadbare carpeting. The coral rattan in their living room curled up at the edges like a patch of wilted grass, and their sleek banana-colored couch, bought in Leonora's first bloom of pregnancy, had turned a shade of ocher over the years. Lacey ran her hand along the polished wooden banister. The walls were painted a gleaming oyster color. There were no fingerprints.

Some quiet time in the bathroom appealed to Lacey. She slipped inside, closed the door, and locked it. An aquatic decorating scheme abounded, with sea-foam walls bordered by a pattern of floating shells, tropical fish, and dancing sea horses. A porcelain bowl of soap in the shape of pink scallops caught her eye. Each perfect shell had a sheen of newness. They sat there like museum pieces, untouched. Lacey resisted the urge to pocket one for good luck.

Going to the bathroom meant that she had to struggle out of her Lycra cat suit, which left her shivering in her bra and underwear, the cat suit in a wad around her feet. She lowered her bare butt onto the toilet and felt a lurch of fear as the doorknob jiggled. Could it possibly be David, searching for her? Had she really locked the door?

"I'll be out in a minute!" she called, crossing her hands over her brassiere as if the doorknob jiggler might burst in at any moment. Lacey finished quickly and dressed, but by the time she had opened the door and stepped outside, the hallway was empty. She wandered into an adjacent bedroom, half expecting to see Rosie and her boyfriend going at it. Instead, Caroline's rhinestone crown shimmered in the light as she kissed the ghoul next to her. Lacey jerked her head back. Unbelievable! Cinderella was busy with somebody who didn't give a hoot about her twitchy eye, and Lacey was left searching for a boy who usually insulted her, who was supposed to bring her a drink she had never wanted in the first place.

Lacey closed the door and tiptoed back down the hallway to the stairs. A flush of warmth spread from her whiskered cheeks to her cat ears. It occurred to her that she knew her destiny now. The handwriting was on the wall. Lacey Monroe Levine was doomed to be a Peeping Tom for the rest of her life.

When she reached the bottom of the stairs, Lacey was tempted to head straight out the door. Tony and Scott McGraw were nowhere to be seen, and Lacey wondered if they were also closeted in some darkened space doing something that Lacey obviously knew very little about, except for an occasional snatch or two of course, and whatever she saw in the movies. Lacey sighed. Maybe it wasn't for her, all that gyrating and saliva and roaming hands. Maybe she would die alone, an eccentric old lady who lavished all her love on a cat. No Vinnies or Davids or Josephs to have and to hold, just a pet or two to keep her company.

"Down the hatch." David startled her as he spoke low in her ear.

"Where have you been?" said Lacey, trying hard to keep the accusatory tone out of her voice. Her father had hated it, she knew, and something deep inside told her that David would hate it, too.

David didn't answer. He flipped the tab on a can of beer and handed it to her. She took the beer and brought it to her lips. The amber brew collided bitterly with the coating of candy corn, but she relaxed the muscles of her jaw and refused to make a face.

David tipped back his head and gulped down half a can.

"Blimey," he said, wiping his mouth with the back of his hand. "That hit the spot."

"I wonder what blimey means," said Lacey, wishing with all her heart that her mother had given her a curfew, except, what good was a curfew if her mother wasn't home to enforce it?

"Blimey means . . ." David hesitated. "Blimey means we should dance," he said, swigging down the rest of his beer and crushing the can in his hand. "Swish!" he said, as he tossed the bent metal basketball-style into a nearby waste-basket. He removed the beer can from her hands and placed it on the table.

The music slowed with miraculous timing as David wrapped his arms around Lacey. She hesitated, surprised by his sudden familiarity and not knowing quite where to wrap her own arms. She clasped his shoulders and they rocked from side to side, David's face buried in her neck. The beery smell, reminiscent of Bob Drew but not as hateful, filled her nostrils. She thought about Rosie vomiting into the toilet bowl, and tried to brush aside the image. She was not supposed to be thinking about Rosie being sick or David's beery breath, was she? Wasn't she supposed to be melting in his arms?

When the song ended, David raised his head and said groggily, "How about going outside?"

Lacey nodded and followed David as he lurched through the kitchen door and out into the back yard. On the patio a wrought-iron table held a cooler full of beer. Lacey's heart sank as he reached for another can. "One for the road," said David as he cracked it open, and he poured the liquid straight down his throat. "C'mere," he said, slinging his other arm around Lacey as he yanked her toward him. "Let's go in there." He pointed to a gazebo at the back of the property, which boasted privacy and darkness and made Lacey's heart race.

They stooped to enter. "Cozy, isn't it?" David said, pulling Lacey next to him as he flopped onto a cold wooden bench. He opened his mouth wide, a giant baby sparrow waiting for his mother to toss a worm inside. Lacey held her breath. Would he speak, or start kissing her? David leaned forward to cover her lips, and she was tasting the remains of his last beer as his tongue took on a life of its own. For some reason the words "Don't drink and drive" kept reverberating in her head, which Lacey knew was ridiculous. As David threatened to tickle her vocal cords, snapshots of happy children, dead and buried and killed by drunk drivers, reeled through her mind. Lacey silently substituted the words "Don't drink and kiss," making a note to herself to share this wisdom with Tony.

Lacey pulled back, not certain if she was breathless from apprehension or lack of air. "Can we talk a little?" she said.

"I love you," said David, nuzzling her neck as he placed a hand between her legs. Lacey stiffened in amazement as the hand ran up and down her thigh like a small rodent foraging for food. It dawned on her that she was impenetrable, a locked vault, a fortress encased in her head-to-toe black spandex cat suit. As David huffed and puffed and nuzzled and snuffled, his hand continued searching for the opening that never appeared. It became frantic, disembodied. David again told her he loved her as his hand traveled along her contours, a racing hand, a speedy hand, skimming Lacey's body as she played the words over and over in her head. "I love you," he said. Stroke, grapple, pinch. "I love you." Nibble, tickle, pull. She could feel her body shrinking, shriveling away from his touch. She realized that she had never felt less loved in her life.

"What is this thing, a trampoline?" David fastened accusing eyes on her.

Lacey began to laugh, a sound that started down in her belly and spiraled into her chest and out her mouth, deep and loud and slightly hysterical, as she mouthed to David, "I want to go home."

8

Lacey ignored the twenty-dollar bill that Leonora had insisted she keep in her pocketbook for emergencies, and walked home in the darkness. This was no emergency. This was the story of her life. David's hand had wandered from base to base on her body, and she had felt absolutely nothing, unless you counted fear and loathing. Her flaky mother spent all her time preening in the mirror, while her older sister did more than that in the basement. Her sister was a sexually active stranger who happened to live in the same house. Her father was a stranger who did not. Even Tony, whom Lacey had discovered dancing with Kenny Lerner, not nesting in a bedroom with Scott McGraw as she had suspected, even Tony hadn't picked up on the gleam of desperation in Lacey's eye that said, "Get me out of here."

"Can you get home on your own?" she had asked.

Lacey could, but she didn't want to. She swallowed her friend's betrayal, her lack of intuition. She called to Tony over the din of the music, "If you need Cinderella, she's upstairs. And I don't know who the hell Prince Charming is." Then she walked out the door.

Prince Charming didn't exist, of course. She hadn't found him, that was for sure. David's drunken "I love you" roared in her ears. She knew in her heart that he would never speak to her, much less call her, never in a million years. She knew now what a combustible mixture booze and words were, and that what that mixture made for was just a bunch of lies.

A string of Halloween decorations lit her way home. She wasn't afraid, just relieved to be walking with a purpose, away from the party, away from David. "I want to go home," she'd told him. What had she expected him to answer? Not "So go." That's what he'd told her. No pleading, no "Let's slow down. Let's get to know each other a little." Just "Go."

Lacey unlocked the front door and entered the silent house. Rosie must have gone to bed. Her mother was out gallivanting. And where the hell was Sherman? Lacey dragged herself up the worn carpeted stairway. She went into the bathroom and focused on the old peeling wallpaper of some obscure summer berry while she brushed her teeth. Leonora's perfume lingered, despite the fact that Rosie had barfed several times.

Lacey entered her sister's bedroom and looked down at Rosie. Pale blond curls swept across her round face, which was warm and flushed and dotted with sweat. She looked ten years old. The quilt was hanging halfway off the bed, and Lacey pulled it up to cover her sister.

"Lacey?" Rosie's voice was young, a little girl afraid of the dark.

"Are you better, Rosie?" Lacey whispered.

"Pretty much," said Rosie, shifting her body toward the wall. "Sit down," she said, patting the bed beside her. "Tell me how the party went."

Lacey nestled next to her sister in the half-light. She hesitated. How could she explain running away from David and his kisses, when her sister ran toward Joseph's?

"So how was it?" persisted Rosie.

"Not so great," Lacey replied, her eyes darting sideways. "Something must be the matter with me."

Rosie slid out from under the covers and propped a pillow under her head. "What happened?"

"Remember David?"

"The guy you have a crush on."

"The jerk I *had* a crush on. He got drunk, and then he got me in a corner and started kissing me and told me he loved me."

Rosie sighed. "And you don't think he loves you," she said matter-of-factly.

"I don't think he'll even remember what happened in the morning."

Yanking the quilt up to her chin and startling Lacey, Rosie fumed, "Why do people have to drink to be cool? That's one thing about Joseph. He hardly ever drinks. Besides, he knows I hate the taste of it."

"As a drink," Lacey said cautiously, "or in his mouth?"

Would Rosie get huffy and refuse to talk? Lacey eased her body under the blanket so that she was against the wall beside her sister. "I mean, have you ever found yourself doing stuff that you never would have done in a million years, but you wanted to please him?" Lacey hesitated. "And then it felt bad?"

"I love Joseph," Rosie said suddenly, her eyes welling up with tears. "I've loved Joseph for a long time."

Lacey looked straight ahead, not at Rosie, as she spoke. "So you couldn't love him and not sleep with him? Is that what happened?"

Rosie took the edge of her sheet and laid it across her eyes. "I was afraid he'd go somewhere else. Get another girlfriend. He kept asking and asking, and I couldn't say no anymore." Rosie gave a strangled kind of laugh from under the covers.

"Why are you laughing?"

"Joseph kept telling me about 'blue balls.' Have you ever heard of that, Lacey? Doesn't it sound awful? He said that if the man has to wait too long, his balls start hurting and actually turn blue."

"What do you mean, his balls turn blue?" Lacey tried to keep her eyes from popping out of her head.

Rosie didn't notice. "And then I read in this magazine that some people say it's a myth. All made up. But it wasn't something that I could really ask anyone about. Dad or someone."

"But you'd . . . you'd already had sex?"

Rosie nodded. "A done deal. And then you can't exactly change your mind and say, I'm not ready. It's like, you've gone through a red light, and you know it's against the law and everything, but you're speeding on the highway by now."

"And what, you couldn't find an exit ramp?"

Rosie leaned her tousled head against Lacey's shoulder. "I told you. I couldn't say no anymore."

"I know," said Lacey. "I mean, I know a little bit what it's like." She remembered David's hands on her, and shuddered.

"I wanted so much for him to be happy," Rosie rambled. "For him not to leave, like . . . For him to stay with me forever."

"For him not to leave, like Daddy. That's what you meant to say, isn't it?"

"What if it is?" Rosie slid down in bed again, uttering a small moan. Finally she said, "I think I'm in trouble, Lacey."

The shrill ringing sound of the telephone interrupted her, and made both girls jump. "Who could be calling us at this time of night?" said Lacey.

"Maybe it's Joseph," said Rosie.

"Or Mom. Maybe Mom's having a guilt trip." Lacey raced into her mother's bedroom and picked up the telephone. "Hello?" she said breathlessly.

"Lacey honey? It's Daddy. I have some exciting news to tell you."

Her father's voice was higher-pitched than usual. Maybe he was moving back home again, Lacey thought. Maybe he had miraculously patched things up with her mother and Leonora was ready to ditch that bodybuilding boyfriend of hers and her father was ready to ditch that snake-in-the-grass new wife of his and they were coming home together. "What news, Daddy?"

"You have a half sister. Her name is Chelsea, and she's beautiful. Almost as beautiful as you were, honey. Seven pounds six ounces, and she has your eyes. Lacey?"

Lacey clung to the telephone, breathing quietly. "Yes, Daddy?"

"When Mommy gave birth to you, you had such dancing eyes. You looked right at me, and I could have sworn you smiled at me. Chelsea did the same thing. She knew right away that I was her father."

"No kidding," said Lacey, pressing the receiver so hard against her ear that it hurt.

"No kidding," her father repeated. "Chelsea Petra Levine."

Lacey cleared her throat. "What's with the Petra?"

Her father chuckled. "I know. I had to give in to Ellie. After fifteen hours of labor, and then a C-section, I couldn't say no. She'll grow into it."

"You mean, you'll get used to it. Why Petra?"

"Ellie's grandmother was named Petra. She died a few years ago."

So did I, Dad, Lacey bellowed in her head. "So congratulations, Dad. She's very lucky to have you."

It was her father's turn to be quiet. "Honey?"

"Yup."

"I love you. This doesn't take away from how I feel about you."

Lacey's eyes brimmed with tears. She held the receiver

away from her and shouted into the hallway, "We have a new sister, Rosie!"

"Are you all right, sweetheart?"

Lacey trembled at the tenderness in his voice. She swallowed the lump in her throat that felt like a giant gum ball and said, "I'm fine, Daddy."

"I know this is hard, honey. Is Mommy there? I'd like to talk to Mommy, too."

"Mommy's not home. She's out on a date."

"So late?"

Lacey laughed into the telephone. "You're not here either, Daddy. We're used to being on our own, you know."

"I'm sorry, you're right," her father said quickly. "Okay, honey. Do you mind getting Rosie for me?"

"Rosie!" Lacey called. "Daddy wants to speak to you."

"I'm sick!" cried Rosie from her bedroom. "Tell him I'm sick."

"She's sick," Lacey told her father. She had the sudden urge to protect him. "She was throwing up before, Dad. It's the truth."

"Then she shouldn't get up. I love you, Lacey. Will you and Rosie come and visit us soon? I'll come and get you."

"Soon, Dad," said Lacey, and hung up the telephone. She left her mother's bedroom and headed back toward Rosie. The bathroom door was shut, and a beam of light shone out the bottom.

"Are you sick again?" Lacey leaned into the doorway. "Do you believe we have a new sister? A half sister. Chelsea Petra Levine. She sounds like a Russian immigrant or something."

Rosie gave an unintelligible answer.

"What did you say, Rosie?"

Rosie's voice was low and desperate. "I'm so afraid, Lacey. You have no idea."

Lacey turned the doorknob and opened the bathroom door. "Afraid of what?" she said.

Her sister was sitting on the tiled floor, her head slung over the toilet seat. "I think I'm pregnant," she said.

9

♥

Lacey rolled into bed without attempting to remove her cat makeup. Most of it was already smudged onto Rosie's pillowcase anyway, and her cat ears were lost somewhere in the bedclothes. She would look for them in the morning.

Lacey was reeling from Rosie's revelation. Her sister, her perfect sister, who always ironed her gym clothes and remembered to water the plants, might be "in the family way." That's what Grandma Pearl had called it when their distant cousin Marla had waltzed solemnly down the aisle in an empire-waist bridal gown that barely disguised her burgeoning form. What was it that Kenny Lerner had said about a senior girl with a protruding belly? Lacey furrowed her brow until it came to her. "Cookin' one in the oven." She could picture him clearly now, snickering into the palm of his hand. Lacey flushed at the thought of it.

Grandma's pronouncement was much more genteel, but it was really no better. She could imagine the winks and raised eyebrows just the same.

Lacey wondered vaguely where Sherman was, and pulled her cat tail close to her chest for comfort as if it were a stuffed animal and she were a little girl. She slid her hand across her flat stomach and pictured it swelling, day by day, until it was as round and ripe as a watermelon. The thought repulsed her. November, December, January, February, March, April, May, June, July. Lacey counted nine months ahead on her fingers, growing time until summer. Shorts and bathing suits and Rosie with a baby in her belly, baking in the oven until it was done. Unimaginable.

Lacey squeezed her eyes shut. *Go to sleep, go to sleep.* Rosie in winter, hiding her pregnancy under baggy clothes. Rosie in April, singing in the Springtime Concert with a stomach the size of Cousin Marla's. *Go to sleep, go to sleep now!* Lacey jerked her head from side to side. Unless of course Rosie had an abortion. But when she had mouthed the word to her sister, Rosie had stared back at her blank-eyed. The next word, marriage, Rosie had rolled around in her mouth as if it were a speck of dirt on a lettuce leaf, or a piece of filling let loose from a tooth.

Lacey pulled the coverlet up to her chin. Her head was swimming, and she was five years old again and waiting for her birthday party to begin. The cake had been iced the night before, the pin-the-tail-on-the-donkey poster was taped securely to the living-room wall, the goody bags were piled in a bowl on the coffee table. Lacey was so excited that she couldn't stop jumping, and when Michael Levine downed his last drop of coffee, he kissed her on the head and called her "my little birthday jumping bean." To his wife, he instructed, "Don't give her too much sugar today. She's wired already."

Leonora didn't mind Lacey's jumping, but she was troubled by her constant head scratching. She made Lacey lay her face on the hard surface of her father's desk, the lamp pulled down so that it illuminated her scalp. Leonora was ruthless, her hand an iron vise around Lacey's skull as she combed and searched and combed some more, while her daughter screeched, "You're hurting me!"

"There's no other way to do this," her mother said, and then she sucked in her breath and said, "Shit. You've got lice."

Lacey had known by her mother's swearing that it was bad. Leonora dragged her into the middle of the living-room floor, plunked her there as if she were a garden gnome, and said, "Stand still, don't touch anything, don't move." Then Leonora gave Rosie the same treatment, head down on her father's desk under the hot desk lamp, until Rosie was screaming. But Rosie's head was clean. Of course.

Leonora had the rest of the morning to call the doctor, buy the medicine, put Lacey in the shower, and scrub her head so hard that her daughter started screeching all over again, and medicinally treat her own head, just in case. Then she did what seemed like a thousand loads of laundry, bagged, tagged, and tied over a hundred stuffed animals that would be prisoners in plastic for several months, and dressed Lacey in her brand-new party dress, her shiny hair all squeaky clean. They waited for the guests to arrive. Except that Leonora had told one mother, who had told another mother, who had told another, and not a single person came to the party. Not even one kindergarten friend or Mark the next-door neighbor or even her cousin Amber. Lacey remembered crying her eyes out, until her father came home. He gathered her onto his lap and kissed the top of her head. "We'll have our own party," he said to Lacey and Leonora and Rosie. Then they all had slices of pizza for supper, and they pinned the tail on the donkey and they lit the candles on the cake and sang the happy-birthday song. Lacey and her father plundered the goody bags later, eating bits of chocolate from one bag or another.

What Lacey remembered best about her birthday was the shame, though, and the thought of "Rosie in bloom" made her own stomach ache. If only Michael Levine could kiss them on the top of their teenage heads now and wave a magic wand and play a party game and make everything all better. Lacey shifted under the covers. Perhaps she should tell her mother, even though Rosie had begged her not to. Lacey imagined it, Leonora home from her hot date with Vinnie, flushed and disheveled and finding out that her darling daughter had been having sex in the basement with Joseph Panteleone and that now she might be pregnant. Leonora would simply roar. She would rant and rave and utter something awful like JOSEPH PANTELEONE SHOULD HAVE KEPT HIS GODDAMNED PANTS ON, AND WHAT THE HELL WERE YOU THINKING? It was all too much for her, the Halloween party and David's hot hands and his drunken I love you's and a brand-new half sister and her mother in la-la-land and her sister getting an abortion or married and in maternity clothes, and Lacey tossed and turned and shuddered and shook before finally drifting off to sleep.

In the morning, Rosie shuffled into the kitchen as Lacey was scraping a heap of wet yellow egg out of a frying pan onto a plate. She looked intently at her sister's face, peered at it closely, searching for the telltale pimple that might announce to the world that Rosie had her period.

But Rosie turned her nose up at the sight of scrambled eggs. "The smell of them makes me feel sick," she said. Her face was clear of blemishes.

"I think we have to tell Ma," Lacey said as though the conversation from the night before had continued uninterrupted into the morning. "We have to get some help."

Rosie's eyes darted up to the ceiling. "Quiet!" she said peevishly. "Don't wake her."

"Then tell Joseph."

"Not yet," said Rosie, shaking her head. "We need to get one of those test kits," she continued. "The kind you see on television, with the plus and minus signs."

"All right," said Lacey, biting into her buttered toast.

"Now," said Rosie, her eyes full of purpose. "We have to do it now, while she's asleep. We can take her car." Rosie stood up and scooped Leonora's keys off the counter. "We'll go to the drugstore in Westfield."

Lacey grabbed her knapsack and a second piece of

toast, and they drove to the pharmacy. Rosie parked the car and they entered the store. They zigzagged up and down the aisles with eyes like radar, zooming in on pregnancy tests, only pregnancy tests, no lipsticks, no aspirin, no body lotion, just pregnancy tests.

"Where are they?" whispered Rosie.

"I'm not asking," said Lacey, but she nearly did a handstand when she spied a counter full of lubricants and suppositories and condoms and spermicides. Next to the prophylactics was a rack of pregnancy tests.

"How handy," Rosie commented as she squinted at the boxes. "If you mess up with the stuff on this side, you can see how bad by picking up one of these."

"This one looks simple enough," said Lacey, holding up a kit.

"Get it," said Rosie. "We need one for morons."

Lacey resisted the urge to hide it under the folds of her jacket. Being arrested for shoplifting a pregnancy test would do nothing for her abysmal weekend. As they stood in line, Lacey's heart started pounding. This was far worse than the purchase of tampons or sanitary napkins in front of a male cashier. She handed the kit to the balding man behind the register and blurted out, "At least Mom can find out if she's pregnant or not. Do you have any money?"

Rosie turned the color of beetroot and fumbled in her purse. "Here," she said vaguely, handing Lacey a five-dollar bill. "Do you need more?"

Lacey rolled her eyes, fishing in her knapsack until she found her wallet. "It's a good thing I have my emergency money with me." She handed the twenty dollars to the cashier, and gave the white pharmacy bag to Rosie.

Rosie tossed her curls and headed for the exit. "If this isn't an emergency, I don't know what is," she muttered.

When they got home, the sisters closeted themselves in the bathroom. Rosie unwrapped the pregnancy test and they read the directions carefully, as if they were baking a cake from scratch. Rosie peed all over her hand as she tried to fill a small cup. Then she poured the urine into a plastic contraption while Lacey set the kitchen timer. They sat down on the bathroom floor and gazed at the plastic container perched on the edge of the bathtub, their oracle, their future.

Rosie turned away and started tracing her index finger around a hexagon-shaped tile. "I can't believe this is me," she whispered, sliding her finger around the six sides of one tile, and then another.

"What happened?" said Lacey as she reached for a grayish sponge nesting in the dust beneath the sink. "This place is filthy, isn't it?"

"What do you mean, what happened?" Rosie stopped her tracing.

"I mean, didn't you use protection?"

Rosie's eyes hardened. "Of course we did. I'm not an idiot, you know."

"I know," said Lacey, standing to wet the sponge. She bent her head and wiped a path of water across the dirty floor. "We need a cleaning woman," she added feebly.

Rosie's laugh was harsh. "You're looking at her, dumbo. I've just had other things on my mind."

The timer made a bell-like sound, echoing loudly in the bathroom.

"Who the hell set the alarm on a Sunday morning?" Leonora shouted from her bedroom.

Rosie smiled grimly and put a finger to her lips. "Shh," she whispered softly. Then she pushed herself up from the floor and brushed off her pants. She approached the container cautiously, as if it were a bomb that needed defusing, and handed it to Lacey. "I can't look," she said, covering her eyes with her hands.

For one brief moment, Lacey was in the back yard running as her sister counted slowly to one hundred. Hide-and-seek, a nice childhood game. She squinted at the container under the dull light coming from the fixture above the sink, kept low in wattage, Lacey suspected, so that her age-conscious mother could face the mirror more easily. Lacey did an about-face and held the container up to the sunlight streaming through the bathroom window. Was the brightness blinding her, or was her heart beating so loud that she was unable to concentrate? Lacey squinted once more and her heart took a nosedive as she announced to Rosie, "It's blue. It's positive."

Rosie sat down on the toilet seat with a flapping sound. "I knew it," she said, laying her face on her outstretched palms.

Lacey heard the muffled sound of sobbing. She bent over her sister and touched her hair. "You don't want Ma to hear," she whispered.

"Did you ever notice how happy they all look?" Rosie lifted her head. "The husband pats the wife's belly, and he's so, so proud?" A tear spilled over the rim of her eye and ran down her cheek as she began to pummel her stomach, slowly and rhythmically, then faster and harder, until Lacey grabbed hold of her hands and said, "Stop!"

"Why?" Rosie said fiercely. "Do you think I'll hurt the baby or something?"

"Don't," pleaded Lacey. "We'll think of something."

Rosie started hiccuping, and covered her mouth once more. "I wanted to go to college," she whispered through her fingers.

"We have to tell somebody," Lacey said desperately. "If you won't tell Joseph, then let me talk to Tony. Tony knows a lot."

"No!" Rosie grabbed a face towel and roughly mopped her cheeks and eyes, and then tossed the cloth into the wastepaper basket.

"You can't throw that away," Lacey chided her sister. She folded the towel and hung it over the rack with the sunflower showing, the way her mother liked it.

Rosie's breath was ragged and uneven. "Sorry, sorry," she said as an afterthought. Her voice took on a steely edge. She said quietly, "I saw a clinic in Plainview, when Joseph and I went to the movies there." Rosie ran the back of her hand across her nose, then wiped its wetness on her trousers. "Will you go with me?"

"Of course I will." Lacey held the container out to her sister. "We don't want this anymore, do we?"

"A souvenir for my scrapbook? I don't think so." Rosie bent to retrieve the white pharmacy bag, and opened it

121

wide. "Put everything in here and I'll throw it outside. Have to get rid of the evidence, don't I?"

Then she stuck her nose outside the bathroom and, bag in hand, ran down the stairs and out the door.

Lacey heard the clanging sound of the lid on the garbage can just as Leonora shuffled into the hallway in her pink bunny slippers, mumbling, "How's Rosie? And how was the party?"

"It was good," said Lacey, "and Rosie's feeling better."

On Wednesday afternoon, Rosie and Lacey boarded the bus to Plainview. The whole day at school, Lacey had felt like a fugitive. She startled quickly and avoided Tony, uttering a brief "I'll call you tonight" as she left her friend in the middle of the hallway and fled out the door.

After Lacey paid the fare, they sat side by side and stared down at their feet for the entire ride. Lacey still felt awkward in her new role as Rosie's leader and protector. She had made the initial phone call to the clinic, found out that it was free to teenagers on Wednesdays, collected change for the bus ride, put the address of the clinic in her pocket, and reminded her sister to bring her calendar, the one that had its numbered blocks marked with the letter P for period. Rosie was a zombie.

They got off the bus on the outskirts of town and walked past the movie house, down a tree-lined side street to a small brick building. Lacey read the name on the eight-inch square sign on the wall. " 'Parenting Institute.' Here we are."

Rosie turned to Lacey, wide-eyed, and whispered, "Can you get an abortion at a parenting institute?"

Lacey ignored her and rang the buzzer. "We have an appointment," she said into the intercom, and at the clicking sound, she pushed open the door.

An enormous lady was seated behind a counter in a chair that groaned and creaked as she wheeled back and forth from computer to file cabinet. "May I help you?" she said, looking straight at Lacey as if she knew that the brunette was the creature of reason, not the wild-eyed blonde beside her.

"We're here to see somebody," said Lacey, gesturing toward Rosie. "I mean, my sister is."

The lady hoisted herself out of the chair, grunting softly as she reached for a wooden clipboard. "And what is your name?" she said.

"Levine," said Lacey, tapping Rosie on the back. "Rose Levine."

"Do you happen to know the first day of your last period, Rose?" At last, the woman focused her eyes on Rosie.

"Yes," she answered tremulously.

"Good." The lady handed the clipboard across to Lacey, four fingers and thumb painted a searing red. "I'll give this to your sister to hold for you, while you go into the bathroom and give me a urine sample." She picked up a pen and, with long tapered fingers that didn't match the undulating flesh of her body, scribbled Rosie's name on a cup. Lacey was mesmerized by the beautiful hands, Barbra Streisand hands, but the red was too much for her, too raucous, too cheerful, too blood-like. It should have been banned from a place like this. Rosie took the cup and let herself into the bathroom, her head turned ever so

123

slightly so that she could catch Lacey's eye. A flicker of fear passed between them.

The bathroom door opened again much too soon and Rosie's head reappeared. "Do I bring it out to you?" she said.

"Just leave it on the silver counter, honey."

The waiting room was furnished in blue, with aqua walls and a darker couch. In the corner of the sofa sat a teenage couple, the girl's head dipping into the crook of the boy's arm, the boy's legs spread wide. The girl had her hands clenched between her skinny thighs, and every once in a while she would draw them out and cup them around her mouth and blow on them.

Lacey was as hot as the girl was cold. She sat sweating across from them before it occurred to her to remove her jacket. The girl was breathing into her hands again, and Lacey found it easier to rest her eyes on the lone female sitting slumped at the other end of the couch. A hank of oily hair hung over her eyes, strategically placed to hide her from the world. Someone new was approaching the waiting room, and Lacey flung her jacket on the empty chair beside her as if she were saving a seat in the movies. In this case, a horror movie. She and Rosie used to love to watch them, hanging on to each other through the grisly bits until the film was over and their father was outside waiting in the car to laugh at their wide eyes and drive them home. This time, Lacey knew, they would board the bus feeling haunted, and home would offer no protection.

Rosie slipped into the chair beside her, draping the

jacket over her knees. "It's cold in here," she whispered. She took the clipboard and started to read.

Lacey leaned over her and skimmed the questionnaire. Name, address, telephone, the clinic's confidentiality statement. Insurance information, date of birth, date of the first day of your last period. Rosie wrote quickly, with the air of a student acing an exam, until the questions began, jarring in their seriousness. "Do you have any sexual concerns?" Rosie lifted her pen in the air for a moment, then wrote down the words, *I'm afraid I might be pregnant.* "What kind of sex do you engage in? Oral__ Anal__ Vaginal__." Lacey looked away as Rosie checked the last choice, but turned back again, transfixed. "How many partners have you had in the last three months?__ The last six?__ The last twelve?__" Rosie's tongue dipped out of the corner of her mouth as she wrote down a number one on the space next to three months. "Have you ever been forced to have sex?" Rosie's eyes flickered as she scribbled a large *no.* "Do you engage in the taking of drugs? LSD__ Marijuana__ Cocaine__ Crack__ Alcohol__. How many times a week? How many times a month?" *Never,* she wrote.

At last Rosie stood, wobbling in place until she could steady herself. Lacey watched her walk over to the counter, her hand trembling as she held the clipboard out to the receptionist.

"The pen, too, honey," said the woman. "We lose dozens every day."

Lacey felt a flash of anger. Didn't the silly woman know that Rosie's life was on the line today, that one single ballpoint pen was of no importance to the world of Rosie Levine? "Oh," said Rosie, patting her empty pants pockets repeatedly until Lacey spied the pen in the corner of her sister's chair and stood up to toss it carelessly onto the counter, so that it rolled off the top and onto the floor.

"Sorry," Lacey called over her shoulder as she sat back down.

Stooping to retrieve it, the receptionist said breathlessly, "The counselor will come and talk to you shortly."

Rosie huddled in her chair while Lacey searched the waiting room for something to read. No beauty-parlor magazines here, no *Cosmopolitan* or *Glamour* or even *Ladies' Home Journal.* No barbershop comic books from the days when they were toddlers and Leonora used to take them to get simple blunt cuts in the red leather barber chairs. No *Newsweek*s or *Time* magazines or *National Geographic*s from their austere dentist's office. No *Highlights for Children.* Just pamphlets on gynecology and good health, and on how to talk to your children about sex.

Lacey read diffidently about breast self-examination and Pap smears and how to keep healthy. Yes, she supposed she ate properly, except for a little too much chocolate when she could get hold of it. Yes, she usually got enough sleep. No, she didn't drink eight glasses of water a day, she would try harder. Okay, she should exercise more frequently, but at least she had already had one routine GYN exam at her mother's insistence.

She read the last sentence in the paragraph twice. "Avoid taking health risks with your mind and body." This was the hardest rule of all, the rule that Rosie hadn't followed, that Lacey could barely fathom these days. Her mind and body did not feel at rest, but what risks had she taken?

She handed the pamphlet to Rosie. Her sister merely placed it on the table in front of her and continued staring at a still-life painting of a bowl of fruit on the opposite wall.

Lacey picked up another pamphlet, this one less clinical. "There are many different ways to give and receive physical pleasure with a partner without engaging in sexual intercourse." Lacey turned the page quickly, but to her disappointment, the pamphlet neglected to tell her how. What a waste. It went on to advise parents to rehearse some ways for the children to say no. Lacey couldn't help smiling. She could picture her mother, pamphlet in hand, saying, "Let's see. There's 'Shit, no!' Or how about 'Get your goddamned paws off of me'? Or 'Don't even think about it, asshole.' " But Lacey suspected that Leonora didn't think they even needed any helpful assertiveness techniques. That after Michael Levine had left, she had shown them by example how to assert yourself and get your life together. She had shown their father, I can survive and thrive without you. Lacey sighed. But her mother had not been given a choice. She had been forced into transformation. Saying no had to do with making choices.

Lacey turned the page and read, "Girls especially need to know that they have the right to say no for any reason at any time no matter how far along the necking or petting has progressed." She could have given the book a great big kiss, then and there. There it was in black and white. She was right to leave David at the party. Because if the cat costume hadn't stopped David, she would have. So what if he would never speak to her again? Necking and petting, for heaven's sake. Lacey snickered to herself. Nobody but Grandma Pearl called it that anymore.

Then the book said, "Don't tell your daughter that the boy will respect you more if you say no. She will respect herself more." Did she respect herself more for leaving David? She supposed she did, but why did she feel so empty? And what about Rosie? Had Rosie totally lost respect for herself?

Lacey glanced over at her sister, who was twirling a strand of hair with her index finger. She looked much more like a three-year-old child than like a girl who had lost respect for herself.

The last paragraph of the manual caught Lacey's eye: "Anyone with doubts about whether he or she wants to enter into a sexual union should wait." Lacey clapped a hand over the hysterical giggle that threatened to escape her mouth. One startled eye grew wider beneath the greasy bangs on the girl in the corner of the couch. Keep calm, stay calm. Rosie had enough troubles of her own without her sister flipping out. Doubts? Did she have any doubts about having sex? She had so many doubts that perhaps it meant that she should wait forever.

"Levine!" someone called.

Rosie and Lacey jumped in tandem as another lady from the clinic approached them, this one thinner, wearing pearly fuchsia lipstick and a smudge of pink blush on each cheek.

"Come with me," Rosie said under her breath as she scrambled to her feet. Lacey followed behind her, her own knees threatening to buckle as they walked into another room and the thin lady closed the door.

"My name is Lorraine Eberhardt," she began gently. "Please sit down."

Rosie sat on her hands at the edge of the seat, her eyes focused expectantly on the counselor's mouth.

"We've run your test, Rose, and the result is positive."

Rosie seemed suspended in the delicate balancing act of slumping into the chair or falling flat on the floor. The counselor's eyes flickered toward the box of tissues. *Is she going to cry?* the woman was thinking, but Rosie shifted back in her chair and spoke plaintively. "What am I going to do?" she said.

Lacey fixed her eyes on the counselor's twin strokes of blush as she moved her face closer to Rosie. "It's going to be okay," she said. "We're going to get through this part, Rose. Shall we talk about your options?"

Rosie nodded her head and continued nodding at intervals as the woman said, "You can continue the pregnancy and raise the baby yourself, or with your parents' help. I see your sister is here for support, isn't she?"

Rosie turned her head from right to left, no, no, no, and the counselor placed a hand on one of Rosie's clenched fists. "These are just options, honey. Nothing I say is engraved in stone." She paused for a moment until Rosie stopped shaking her head, then spoke slowly and clearly. "We can help you to terminate the pregnancy, Rose. The next step would be for you to come in and have a pre-abortion exam. Then, a day or two later, you would come in for the termination." The lady's eyes darted down to Rosie's questionnaire. "From the date of your last period, I see that you're just a few weeks along, Rose. We like to stay under ten weeks here." The lady looked questioningly at Rosie, then at Lacey. Rosie was frozen in place.

"I guess she isn't sure," Lacey interpreted. "Is that it, Rosie?"

"Yes," said Rosie miserably.

"I understand." The woman hesitated. "Rose, another possibility would be for you to continue the pregnancy and place the baby for adoption."

Rosie's nostrils flared slightly, and she said, "You mean give the baby away?"

The woman nodded. "Or you could continue the pregnancy and marry the baby's father. I see by your chart that you know who the father is, Rose." Her hand went out, a nail-bitten hand without a hint of polish, pushing the box of tissues toward Rosie.

Had the counselor seen a glimmer in the corner of Rosie's eye, or was it simply time for the client to cry? Rosie took a tissue and dabbed at the stream of tears that coursed down her face. "I know who he is," she whispered. "He . . . I don't know. I don't know if he's . . ." Rosie's shoulders started shaking. She raised a hand awkwardly and fumbled in the tissue box for a wad an inch thick that she held across her wet face.

"You have a little bit of time, Rose. Why don't you go home and think about all of this? I'll be here if you need to speak to me about anything we've discussed. Okay?"

"Okay," said Rosie, barely audible, gulping hard into the tissues.

Lacey caught hold of her sister's arm and helped her to her feet as if she were an invalid. Rosie stood weakly, clutching the sheaf of papers that the counselor had given her. They followed Lorraine Eberhardt in a funereal march out the door.

The bus was packed with commuters on the way home. Lacey and Rosie hung on to a greasy pole, crushed between the knees of seated passengers. Holding on to the next pole down was a hugely pregnant woman, her large belly rocking as the bus sped over potholes, a belly that looked as if it would pop at any moment. The seated commuters guiltily avoided looking at her, lest they have to give up their seats for her. They hunched in their spaces, staring mindlessly at posters. But Rosie saw her and shuddered.

Lacey turned away and caught sight of a clean-shaven man with a chiseled jaw who reminded her of her father. She surprised herself by welling up with tears. Perhaps they could go for a visit this weekend, before Rosie had to make up her mind. Perhaps he *would* kiss them both on the tops of their heads and make everything all better. Or perhaps Rosie would tell her father, and Lacey would be free again, free to agonize over her own life instead of her sister's.

When the bus reached their stop, Rosie jumped up

first and pushed open the back doors. It encouraged Lacey, as if the act of leaving the bus without help meant that Rosie could actually make a decision about her life.

They walked home briskly in the winterish air, hands jammed in their pockets, heads bent.

Rosie spoke once. "A little bit of time doesn't seem like a lot, does it?"

"It's not," said Lacey.

10

♥

For the next twenty-four hours or so, Lacey ignored her sister. It felt easier that way. How did the saying go? *Denial isn't just a river in Egypt.* For a little while, Lacey pretended that life was back to normal again. After all, she had helped her sister as much as she could, and in the end it was Rosie who had to make the decision.

Whether denial was just a river in Egypt or not, Lacey was still the only vessel adrift in the water. It had been hard for her to talk to Tony lately, since she couldn't tell her what was really on her mind. Leonora was out of the question, and Grandma Pearl was her daughter's staunch ally. As for Lacey's father, he was minding a baby of his own.

Tony had called that very evening and grilled her like a detective. "Where did you disappear to this afternoon?"

Lacey faltered for a moment and then blurted out the

lie that she had carefully prepared. "I saw David coming down the hallway, and I couldn't face bumping into him."

"It's his loss, Lacey. He's the one who got plastered. Why should he take it out on you?"

Lacey sighed. "He's not exactly taking it out on me," she said. "He's pretending I don't exist."

"I'm not going to say, 'I told you so,' said Tony, laughing. "Once a jerk, always a jerk. So where did you rush off to with Rosie?"

"We went to the dentist," Lacey said, grateful that Tony couldn't see her face.

"Any cavities?"

"None at all." Lacey got off quickly before she had to make up something else. Tony's "I'm in your corner" camaraderie was what she loved best about her friend. She never judged Lacey, never asked her why she had run away from David. She defended Lacey against the world. But how would Tony feel about Rosie?

It was as though she were living inside a secret that was swelling in the darkness like the beginnings of the baby in Rosie's belly, except that the secret had taken on a form of its own. It was ready to fly out of Lacey's mouth, splinter into a thousand pieces, find a home somewhere else. And if it was difficult not telling Tony, it was even harder not telling her mother.

At dinner that night, Leonora said, "If you don't start eating again, Rosie, I'm taking you to the doctor."

Lacey could barely stop herself from shouting, "Been there, done that, Ma." She shoveled a spoonful of rice into her mouth, ruling out remarks as they richocheted in her head. "She could be putting on quite a bit of weight soon, Mother," would be a conversation stopper. Or how about "Would you prefer that she eat for two?"

Leonora hiked her sleeve up to her elbow, clenching her teeth as she contracted a bicep. "I bought some weights, girls, and I think I'm seeing a difference already. What do you think?" She fingered the soft flesh under her upper arm. "I'm trying to get rid of this loose part," she explained.

"Grandma Pearl has a lot of that," said Rosie, pushing a lump of brown rice from one side of her plate to the other. "It's gross."

"We used to play with it," added Lacey. "Remember? Grandma used to hold out her arm and we'd make it jiggle. Pretty disgusting."

Leonora pulled down her sleeve. Slowly, delicately, she resumed eating. "Thank you so much for sharing, girls," she said between her second and third mouthfuls. "Your support is appreciated."

"You're welcome," said Lacey, shrugging.

"Forget about it, Mom," said Rosie. "Yours isn't anywhere near as bad as Grandma's."

Lacey shot her a look. She couldn't believe Rosie was still playing the good girl. Lacey steeled herself against the shroud of guilt that threatened to descend on her. Too bad if her mother's feelings were hurt. Lacey felt as though her own life had fallen through the cracks, like pieces of money, the odd penny here, a nickel there, that slid between the cushions and settled in the dust. It would have been nice to talk about her own garbage for a change instead of her mother's or Rosie's. And loose flesh swinging from her mother's forty-something arm was nothing compared to a big fat belly on a small blond seventeen-year-old.

Bob Drew had telephoned earlier in the week, and by Saturday, Lacey was getting ready to babysit again. Divorce was not imminent, she supposed, throwing a novel into her knapsack in case there was nothing good to watch on television.

Her mother was at the gym today, working out with a trainer who had been handpicked by Vinnie. When Leonora had trounced down the steps wearing a brand-new outfit—a unitard, for heaven's sake—Lacey had rolled her eyes.

"What?" said Leonora, hands on her Lycra-clad hips. "What the hell is that for?"

"Stop trying so hard," said Lacey. "You'll never be seventeen again, Ma."

"It's called staying fit," flashed her mother. "What do you want from me? Do you want me to be one of those mothers who get fat and grouchy and go around in baggy sweatpants all day long?"

"Heaven forbid," said Lacey, her voice oozing sarcasm. "Forgive me for criticizing my mother, the jock." She took one look at Leonora's face, etched with fury, and went no further. Leonora trounced out of the house without another word.

It was all too ridiculous, like a sound bite from one of the talk shows Leonora used to watch: "My Mother

Doesn't Act Like a Mother Anymore," or something like that. Lacey pictured a stage full of daughters complaining that their mothers were dating men half their age, and then some sleazeball mama sashaying down a runway in a short leather skirt with most of her butt showing. The whole audience would groan, and when the mother finally smiled, the *pièce de résistance,* half her teeth would be missing.

Lacey had no doubt that Leonora was losing it. A personal trainer. A *body sculptor!* For what? To tone up her figure so that she would look better in bed? Lacey swept the alarming thought out of her head. Why couldn't her mother be dating a respectable older person like Mr. Livingstone? She could go bird-watching with him, or bake him a dozen oat-bran muffins to keep him regular. And Mr. Livingstone would be perfectly happy to see an untoned Leonora in a long flannel nightgown, for heaven's sake.

Lacey sat down and waited on her mother's new seafoam green sofa. Another post-Vinnie purchase that Leonora had made. First her body and now her house was getting a total overhaul. Except that their sleek, discolored, ten-year-old couch had been replaced by a plump, pillow-fat sofa, and Leonora's rounded femininity was being streamlined by some personal trainer into middle-aged bonyness. Lacey sank into the soft feather ticking. Patting the pillow beside her, she called out, "Sherman! Where are you, Sherman?" She heard the tiniest mewing sound, and sat very still. A distant squeak issued from the bookshelves, and Lacey crossed to the other side of the living room. She zeroed in on the noise. Removing a collection of Arthur Miller plays, Lacey found Sherman stretched behind the remaining books.

"Come here, you silly cat," she said, scooping her up and depositing her in front of a bowl of food in the kitchen. "I haven't seen you in ages."

Sherman gave the kibble a sniff, turned tail, and trotted ahead of Lacey into the living room. She jumped effortlessly from floor to stereo speaker, from speaker to bookshelf, and slid behind another row of books.

The front door slammed so hard that the lighting fixture in the dining room trembled on the ceiling. Lacey looked into her sister's red-rimmed eyes and knew.

"You told Joseph, didn't you?" she said.

"I told him, all right. He nearly had a heart attack." Rosie slumped down on the couch, her head tucked against her chest, so that a tiny double chin formed.

"What did he say?"

"He said I have to get an abortion."

"That's it?"

"That's it. No ifs, ands, or buts." Rosie patted her stomach three times for emphasis.

"So are you going to?"

"I have to get the exam first, on Monday."

"He'll go with you?"

Rosie sighed. "I guess so."

"So it's settled?" Lacey searched for the right words. What could she say to her sister? You're making the right decision? Whatever feels right to you? You'll be glad when it's over? Lacey certainly would be. She gathered up her knapsack, grateful to hear the sound of honking outside. "Gotta go, Rosie," she said at last.

Lacey hesitated at the doorway, giving her sister a final look. There was a numbness about Rosie that made her uneasy, as if her sister's body were shot full of novocaine. "Are you sure you'll be all right?" she said, her hand on the doorknob.

Rosie raised her head, one pink cheek marred by a single tear. "There's nothing else I can do, is there, Lacey? This is the only way, don't you think?" She rubbed her stomach absentmindedly, or was it some innate protective measure brought on by pregnancy?

"I don't know what to say," said Lacey.

"Go." Rosie raised a limp hand and waved her away. "Go babysit."

Lacey stepped outside, breathing long and hard as she sucked air into her lungs. It was cold and fresh and spread through her whole body and felt wonderful. As she let herself into Bob Drew's car, she realized that what she was actually feeling was something else: relief. Relief that she could concentrate on her own bullshit life now.

When Jason opened the door, he was tapping a pair of wooden sticks on the drum that hung around his neck. "I have a drum!" he said gleefully, banging his sticks for emphasis.

Lacey rumpled his familiar head. He was so uncomplicated, so single-minded. "I have a drum," he said. No life decisions here, no abortions or marriages or urine samples or sex, just playing with toys and eating ice cream and watching a favorite television show.

"I left our number on the kitchen table," said Karen Drew, adjusting an earring.

"We may be late," warned her husband. "We're meeting friends who moved way out in the sticks."

Lacey closed the door behind them and began the business of babysitting, marching behind Jason with the tambourine he gave her, playing Chutes and Ladders for all of five minutes, then a very noisy game of hide-and-seek so that Jason would find her immediately.

"Where are you going?" Jason called as she walked out of the living room.

"I'm going to the bathroom," Lacey told him.

Jason chortled. "I don't wear a diaper anymore."

"Me neither," Lacey answered, smiling to herself as she heard him laugh.

A crashing sound from the kitchen made her heart jump. She leaped to her feet, pulling up her blue jeans as fast as she could and racing out of the bathroom. Jason stood motionless in the hallway, one pudgy index finger pointing toward a spreading orange liquid on the kitchen floor.

"What happened?" said Lacey, picking him up as he edged toward the puddle.

"I wanted juice," said Jason, his eyes welling up with tears. "Mommy says I'm a big boy."

"You are a big boy," said Lacey, settling him onto the living-room couch. "But that was one big container of orange juice, and I have to go clean it up now. At least it wasn't glass."

"Mommy's going to be mad at me," he called plaintively after her. He started crying.

"Mommy doesn't have to know," said Lacey, pulling a plastic bag out of the cupboard and setting it down next to the flood. She went through two rolls of paper towels, wiping and tossing into the bag, until the floor was cleared of juice but tacky to the touch. Lacey opened up the cabinet underneath the sink and peered inside. Mr. Clean, Lysol, window cleaner with ammonia.

Jason appeared next to her. "Mommy uses that one," he said, pointing to a container. "I can help."

Lacey handed him a few squares of towel. "I'll spray and you wipe," she said, sitting back on her heels.

When the task was completed, Lacey said, "Let's get rid of the evidence. Your mom will never know what happened." It occurred to Lacey that secrecy was beginning to feel familiar to her. Hiding things from mothers, including her own, was becoming her specialty.

Jason started to giggle, happy to be part of the secret as he gathered up the paper bag full of garbage. "I know where it goes," he said, darting into the living room and squeezing the bag to his body as he grasped the doorknob.

"Out here," called Jason as he ran into the hallway.

"Where are you going?" Lacey yelled after him, following him down the corridor. The thud of the door as it slammed to a close echoed in her head.

She knew immediately that they were locked out of the apartment, but she walked slowly back to the door, took hold of the doorknob, and turned it hopefully. It didn't budge.

"Terrific," she said, retracing her steps toward the incinerator, where Jason was attempting to open the chute.

"I can't do it," he said. "It goes down here."

Lacey opened the chute and pushed the overflowing paper bag into it. She turned to examine her charge.

At least he was wearing warm pajamas and slippers. Lacey was grateful for anxious parents like the Drews, worried about bare feet and splinters, short sleeves and sniffles.

As for herself, Lacey was thankful that she'd worn a sweatshirt, but kicked herself for not having so much as a quarter in her pocket to make a phone call.

"We're locked out of the apartment," she said casually to Jason. "Does anyone else have a key?"

"Grandma," said Jason. "Grandma has one."

"Do you remember Grandma's phone number?" Lacey asked him.

"Press 'one' on the phone," he said.

"We can't get to your phone," said Lacey, squatting down so that she could look him straight in the eye. "Is Mommy friendly with anyone in the building?"

"Mr. Goldsmith," said Jason. "He sews Mommy's clothes."

"Let's go downstairs to the lobby," said Lacey, taking him by the hand and leading him into the elevator.

"I'll push the button," Jason said happily.

When the elevator doors opened, Lacey followed Jason into the vestibule and skimmed the names for Mr. Goldsmith.

"3D," she said, her finger on the buzzer. She waited several seconds.

"He's not home," said Jason. "Should I try another button?"

"Let me think," said Lacey, panic rising in her voice. "It's too far to walk to my house, and I don't even have *my* house keys with me."

Jason's mouth dipped. He squinted up his eyes, examining her face for signs of worry.

"We're fine," Lacey said hastily. "We'll just sit here for a few minutes while I think of something."

They parked themselves on a bench next to a bedraggled potted plant, the only attempt at decoration in the lobby. An older couple entered the building, intent on conversation. Lacey summoned up the courage to say something but shut her mouth quickly. How could she ask two total strangers if she and Jason could wait in their apartment for several hours? It was all too terrible. Jason took his two small fists and started rubbing his eyes, a sure sign that he was about to cry. Instantly, Lacey began singing nursery rhymes, her warbly voice full of fake cheerfulness. The little boy jumped out of his seat, hopping from tile to tile in time to "Jack and Jill went up the hill."

A familiar voice interrupted Lacey just as she finished the verse about fixing Jack's head with vinegar and brown paper. "I have a question for you."

"Hi, Rob!" Jason called brightly as he sprawled to a stop at Rob's feet.

"Hey, big guy," said Rob, smiling at Lacey as he ruffled Jason's hair. "Tell me something, Jase. How do you fix a broken head with vinegar and brown paper?"

Lacey smiled back, despite the fact that she was stranded in a hallway with no place to go. "Maybe that's how they used to make Band-Aids in the olden days," she said.

"I'm Jack and Jill," Jason piped up.

"You've got to be Jack," Rob said, laughing. "You look too macho to be Jill."

"What's macho?" said Jason.

"Like a man. You look like a man."

"Daddies have penises and mommies have *baginas.*"

"What have you been teaching him?" said Rob, widening his eyes at Lacey. "This is some babysitter you've got, Jason."

Lacey opened her mouth to defend herself, when Rob asked the question, "What are you two doing lurking in the hallway?"

"It's a long story," Lacey began. "I was in the other room and . . ."

Jason cut in. "She was making peepee."

"I was not!" Lacey blushed as Jason rushed on with his explanation.

"Uh-huh. Remember? You said you didn't need a diaper anymore."

"She did, did she?" said Rob, eyeing her. "I'm very proud of you, little girl."

"Stop!" said Lacey, grinning broadly as she covered her ears.

Jason cut in again. "I spilled the whole bottle of juice all over the floor. Lacey said we could hide it from my mommy."

"A bit of subterfuge, eh?" said Rob, raising an eyebrow. "Please go on, young man."

"We hid it," said Jason solemnly. "The *ebidense.*"

"The evidence?" said Rob. "You hid the evidence?"

Jason shook his head up and down quickly. "We got locked up."

"Knocked up?" asked Rob. "Did you say knocked up?"

Lacey's heart skipped a beat as she examined Rob's smiling face. "Locked out," she corrected, aware that her cheeks were burning. Lacey pulled Jason into her lap and peered over his head into Rob's eyes. "We're locked out of the apartment," she said, her voice rising. "What are you doing here, anyway?"

"I live here," said Rob. "Come on up with me, and we'll figure out what to do."

Lacey set Jason down on the floor and they both followed Rob toward the elevator. He took his time walking, which gave her a few moments to get a good look at him. Lacey smiled to herself as she realized that she had only seen him from the waist up at the deli counter. She made a note to tell Tony what a great butt he had.

"We're going to Rob's *bapartment?*" said Jason, bright-eyed.

"You're going to my *bapartment,*" said Rob, laughing as he pushed the button for the elevator.

"His mother doesn't want me to imitate his mistakes," said Lacey, rolling her eyes. "She wants me to correct him so he can learn the right word."

Rob gave her a knowing look. "I think we heard some of the right words before, didn't we?"

Lacey giggled as he bent low and waved her into the elevator with a flourish. "To Oz?" he said, dipping his voice like the Scarecrow.

"To Oz," said Lacey, smiling widely again. "I just love that movie."

"Me, too," said Jason, running ahead of her. "Let's watch it."

"We could, actually. We have the tape," said Rob, pressing a button. He turned to face the two of them. "Now, staff," he said, sounding brisk and businesslike. "I've called you all here for this meeting because . . ."

Lacey stared at him, blank-eyed.

"It's a joke," Rob said, shaking his head sadly. "Not a very good one."

"Not very good," Jason agreed.

"Yes, it is," said Lacey, recovering.

"I won't quit my day job," Rob said, grinning as the door slid open. He waited until Jason and Lacey passed him, calling out "Number 5D" as Jason sped down the hallway.

"Slow down," yelled Lacey. "That's what got us into trouble in the first place."

"You locked us up," said Jason as Rob ushered them into the apartment.

"She locked you out," Rob corrected him, glancing sideways at Lacey. "See? I'm teaching him like you told me to." He hung his keys on a hook on the wall. "I know what it's like to get locked out, Jase. My dad put this here because I was losing my keys so much."

"I didn't lock us out," Lacey said grouchily. "I ran after

you, and the door slammed shut." Lacey plopped down next to Jason on the couch. "I can't believe I did that," she said miserably. "They're going to be so mad at me."

"It wasn't your fault," said Rob. "Want some tea?"

"I want chocolate milk," said Jason.

"No chocolate milk," Lacey said sharply. "Chocolate will keep you up. Have some regular milk." She softened her voice as she turned toward Rob. "Tea sounds good," she said.

Rob strode into the kitchen, calling over his shoulder, "You're lucky, Jase. When I was little, my babysitter looked like the witch in *The Wizard of Oz*. Yours is pretty, like Dorothy."

The refrigerator door opened and shut as Lacey's cheeks grew pinker. She heard water running, then the click of the gas burner on the range top and the sound of the teakettle hitting metal.

"Here you go," said Rob, avoiding Lacey's eyes as he handed Jason a plastic thermos with a built-in straw. He crouched in front of the television set, pulling out a tape, peering at the label, and replacing it. Lacey could see the band of his underwear, Fruit of the Loom briefs that reminded her of her father, and a patch of skin above it.

Judy Garland appeared on the screen, singing "Somewhere Over the Rainbow" with such hope and yearning that when Dorothy's eyes filled with tears, Lacey's, to her horror, did the same. *Get a grip,* she told herself, wiping quickly at her eyes with her index fingers. She remembered sitting next to her father, just the way Jason was nestled next to her. He sipped on his milk with such a look of pure contentment that Lacey felt her eyes well up with tears all over again.

When the song was over, Jason whispered into her shoulder, "Stay with me when the witch comes, okay, Lacey?"

"Of course I will, honey," said Lacey, bending over to kiss him on the top of his head. "I'll be next to you the whole time." Her father had told her the same thing, and where was he now? Rocking Chelsea Petra Levine.

Rob set two cups of tea in front of her on the coffee table. "I wrote this note," he explained, pulling a piece of paper out of his pocket. "It says, 'We got locked out of the apartment and are waiting for you at Rob Lyon's, Apartment 5D. Don't worry.' Is that okay? Should I go tape this on their door?"

"That's fine," said Lacey. "Thanks, Rob."

"Can I get you anything else?"

"Milk," said Lacey. "Milk for my tea."

"Coming up," said Rob, bounding back into the kitchen so quickly that Lacey started to laugh.

Rob returned, a dishrag draped over his arm as he bent to pour milk into her teacup.

"Madam," he said. "Have you any other needs?"

"None, Niles," said Lacey, wondering where she got the name from. "Your mother taught you well, young man."

"She did," said Rob. "Always be a gentleman, she told me."

"I can't hear," said Jason. "Be quiet!"

"Pushy young tot," said Rob. "I'm just going to put this

note on your door, so your mom and dad know where to find you."

When he returned, Jason said, "Sit down next to Lacey." She shifted closer to the little boy as Rob sank into the couch beside her, one knee brushing against her own.

"Sorry," he said, moving it inches away from her.

"It's okay," said Lacey, but she had liked his touch. As the Tin Man and Dorothy, the Scarecrow, and the Cowardly Lion knocked on the gated doors to the palace, Lacey realized how well Rob's mother had taught him. Not a single part of his body, not a hand or a leg or a knee or an elbow, came near her for the rest of the movie.

Jason, however, was slumped against Lacey, his arms wrapped around her, snoring contentedly.

11

♥

Karen Drew scooped up Jason and bundled him out of Rob Lyon's apartment as if her son were in imminent danger of catching an incurable disease. She held him to her chest and hunched her shoulders so that neither Jason nor she touched a wall or a piece of furniture, and then scuttled out the door and down the corridor.

Bob Drew trained his eyes on Lacey's forehead, lecturing her on the dangers that could have befallen them. He ignored Rob completely.

Rob responded by deliberately keeping Mr. Drew outside his immediate sphere of vision. He cleared the dishes, wiped down the coffee table, straightened couch pillows, corrected the angle of a framed picture while *The Wizard of Oz* was rewinding.

Bob Drew held his face inches from Lacey now, gathering steam as he admonished that she and Jason could have frozen to death, that someone could have abducted them, that Jason could be severely traumatized. Lacey stifled a nervous titter as her nose experienced trauma of its own—the combined stench of garlic and beer, like the air from some foul-smelling hair dryer fired at her nostrils. She drew back. He followed, maintaining the odious six inches from her face.

At the click of the VCR, Rob popped the tape back into its box and commented quietly, "Jason had a good time."

Bob Drew appeared not to hear. "I'll take you home," he addressed Lacey, sweeping past Rob in a final display of disapproval. Lacey paused briefly, tapping Rob's arm gently with her fingers before following behind Mr. Drew.

"See you," Rob mouthed softly to her.

"Bye," she whispered back, turning her head for a last look at the lanky body that slouched against the doorjamb, his hair as tousled as Jason's. He nodded back at her, giving her a slightly pained look as if he were in some way responsible for Lacey's troubles. She wondered vaguely if he resembled his father, who didn't want him to lose his keys, or his mother, who had taught him to behave like a gentleman.

As they drove home, not a single mention was made of Bob Drew's cousin who would have loved to take her out. Lacey's accidental lockout had translated into putting their precious son in harm's way. She was damaged goods now.

Instead, Mr. Drew expounded some more. "We don't

know anything about this Rob kid. Just that the three of them moved into the apartment building a few years ago, and then the mother died. Cancer, I think. The kid's in and out of the building, hangs around like a derelict. The father's always working." Bob Drew slammed on his brakes as a carload of teenagers cut into the lane in front of him. "See what I mean?" he said, as if the incident confirmed Rob's worthlessness.

"His mother is dead?" She couldn't decide if the clutch in her stomach was from the seat belt digging into her flesh or from the newfound knowledge that Rob had no mother. It pained her. Yet he had let Lacey speak about her as if she were alive and well, teaching her son about making tea for company and polishing the coffee table and treating girls with respect. No wonder the home was decorated in shades of brown and tan and gold. Boy colors. His mother had died and Rob's father was out working and he was home, eating supper alone, playing music by himself, doing homework with the constant buzz of a radio to round out the emptiness. Grieving. She'd heard the apartment sounds that kept him company, the lady he called "the late-night neat freak" who lived above him and vacuumed at ten o'clock in the evening, the family below him that blasted the television, some kids in the hallway who bounced a few balls until a crotchety old man emerged from next door and put a stop to it.

"He works at the deli," Lacey spoke abruptly. There. Surely she had cleared Rob's name of derelict behavior. Didn't holding down a steady job prove to Bob Drew that he wasn't a goof-off?

Bob Drew was driving like a maniac now, and Lacey flattened against the car window as they careened around the corner, a block from her house, she realized with a start. Extracting the house keys from her knapsack as quickly as she could, she waited for Bob Drew's rebuttal.

"It figures that he works at the deli," he replied, pulling the car up to her house. "It's a hangout, isn't it? I tell Karen not to go there. They charge an arm and a leg for a half gallon of milk and you can hardly get in the door with all the kids crowding around the entranceway."

Lacey unbuckled her seat belt and opened the car door.

"Let's think about next week," Mr. Drew said, tossing the words at her as she let herself out.

"Jason ran out of the apartment," said Lacey, leaning into the car. "I had no idea where he was going, so I had to follow him. But he was never scared, and he didn't cry once."

"You never leave an apartment before making sure you have the keys."

"I have to go," said Lacey, regretting that she had bothered defending herself. She slammed the car door and hurried up the walkway. Her house key slid compliantly into the lock and she uttered a "thank you" to it. People made mistakes, didn't they? When she was little, she would never have predicted that her parents would divorce. Never ever *ever*. They used to slow-dance in the living room until Rosie and Lacey slipped inside their circle of arms and danced along with them. Then her father had made a mistake and the circle had been shattered. How did her mother put it? He should have looked the other way. And what about Rosie? Rosie used to be a virgin, for heaven's sake.

Leonora's car was parked in the driveway. Surprise, surprise, her mother might actually be home tonight. Unless of course Vinnie Rizzo had picked her up for an adventure at his house, pinching various parts of Leonora's flesh to see if the weight training was working. Lacey grimaced at the unthinkable vision of her mother and Vinnie in a tangle of limbs like the one she'd seen her sister and Joseph in. But she had to admit that Leonora was happier than she had been in a long time. And Lacey had a mother, alive and well. Rob did not.

Lacey sighed. As long as Vinnie Rizzo didn't turn up at the breakfast table for some whole-wheat pancakes, she supposed she'd have to put up with him.

The smell of marinara sauce permeated the house. Someone had eaten a late dinner, more likely Rosie than Leonora. Her mother's latest fitness rule was no consumption of food after six o'clock, because, she said, it was harder to work off the calories. Lacey threw her knapsack into the corner of the hallway before entering the kitchen. Two bowls smeared with spaghetti sauce sat on the counter, glasses flanking them. Perhaps Joseph had been there, the unwed father who only came around the Levine residence when Rosie was alone. The coward. Then again, perhaps not. The night before, Lacey had overheard Rosie yelling into the telephone, "What do you mean, *you have needs?* You have *got* to be kidding me, Joseph!" Then she had slammed down the telephone, uttering a Leonora-like "Asshole!" before running to her room.

Rosie had left a note on the kitchen table. "Dad called and wants us to visit. I told him next weekend should be good. Rosie."

Next weekend should certainly be good. On Monday, Rosie would see the doctor and have her examination, and on Tuesday she would have the abortion. Would she be better by the weekend? Lacey crumpled up the piece of paper and threw it into the garbage can. Sherman's dish lay next to it, a darkish scab covering the untouched mound of food.

"Here, puss puss, come to me, puss puss," Lacey chanted. "Come and eat your food, Shermie." She listened intently, then backtracked into the living room to check the bookshelves, but the cat was nowhere to be found. Lacey sank into the sofa and trained her eyes on the fraying carpet. If she looked carefully, she thought, she might be able to see the old etched pattern of her family's dancing feet.

On Monday morning, Lacey woke to the sound of her mother screaming. She clambered out of bed and ran barefoot down the steps.

Leonora was bending over the sofa, her nose an inch from the upholstery.

"What on earth is the matter, Ma?"

Her mother pointed at an expanse of cushion, crying, "What the hell is that?"

Lacey examined the thin pinkish trail that wound its

155

way across the sea-foam green fabric, from pillow to pillow, until it formed a slimy ski slope down the front of the couch.

"There's some on the floor, too," said Lacey in hushed tones. "Where's Rosie?"

"What the hell difference does it make where Rosie is?" Leonora said shrilly. "Where's Sherman?"

"Sherman?" Lacey said dumbly. She peered once more at the stain, her heart leaping in her chest as she realized that her mother might be right. It was the cat, not Rosie, who had left a trail of sickness across her mother's brand-new couch.

"Help me find her," said Leonora.

"Sherman?"

"Of course, Sherman," said her mother, wild-eyed. She sank to her knees, bending at the waist to look under the sofa. "Sherman?" she cried. "Son of a *bitch!* Sherman! Come out here this minute!"

"I don't think she's going to come if you call her like that," said Lacey.

"Because she knows I'm going to kill her." Leonora stood up quickly. "What is it, Lacey? I don't deserve to have anything nice in my life? I don't deserve anything clean and new and pretty and . . ." Her mother sputtered to a stop.

"Sherman didn't do it on purpose, Ma. She's sick." Lacey walked over to the wall of bookshelves and tilted her head sideways. "She's been hiding behind here lately," she whispered, examining one section of books at a time. "There she is."

"Get her for me," said Leonora. "I'm taking her right to the vet."

"Here, puss puss," said Lacey, grabbing a handful of books and putting them on the coffee table. She scooped up Sherman and handed her to Leonora.

"Get me the cat carrier," her mother commanded. "It's in the basement."

Lacey switched on the cellar light and ran down the steps. She avoided looking too long at the cot, which was folded closed, leaning against the cement wall. Her eyes darted from barrel to box as she searched for the cat carrier. "I can't find it," Lacey called, just as she caught sight of it in the corner by the washing machine.

She lugged the cat carrier up the stairs and set it down on the floor by her mother. "Where's Rosie?" she repeated, bending to open the wire door of the cage.

"At Glee Club practice. She left early." Leonora put the squirming cat through the opening and fastened the door shut. Squinting at her watch, she said, "I'm taking her straight to the doctor's before she makes a mess somewhere else." Leonora paused at the front door. "Lacey?"

"Yes, Mom." Lacey waited for her mother to apologize.

Leonora gazed at the couch for a moment, then addressed her daughter. "What the hell gets blood out of upholstery?" she said.

"Maybe Grandma will know," said Lacey, shaking her head. "I'll call her."

Grandma Pearl's answering machine had clicked on when Lacey telephoned. Lacey remembered something about seltzer, but she had finished the bottle the day before. Hairspray was good for some kind of stain, but she wasn't sure what. Ice helped with gum, she was pretty certain of that. Lacey opted for cleaning the material with soap and water and a toothbrush. It seemed the safest way to go, and her mother would obviously flip if she added a hairspray stain to what was already there.

She saturated the couch with warm water, scrubbing her way along the length of the stain to the beat of a reggae song, until the disc jockey announced the time. It was late. Lacey threw on her coat and left the couch with its long wet patch to dry.

Lacey slipped into homeroom seconds after the bell rang.

"What's up?" said Tony, wagging a shaming finger at her. "You're late."

"An emergency cleaning job," said Lacey, sniffing at her fingers. "Ooh, gross, the cat made a mess all over my mother's new couch, and I didn't even have time to wash my hands."

"Lovely," said Tony. "A new perfume. Leonora is not very happy, I'm sure."

"She wasn't," Lacey said flatly. "Happiness doesn't live in our household lately."

Tony raised an eyebrow. "Very metaphorical or something, I'm sure."

"I mean, what exactly has been going *right* in my life, Tony? Can you think of a single thing?"

"I thought your babysitting job had definite possibilities, including a very cute butt."

Lacey laughed in spite of herself, realizing with a start what a foreign act it had become. She'd spent the whole day Sunday with her sister, moping around the house, waiting for the next day and then the day after that to arrive so that Rosie's life could return to normal. That's how Rosie had put it. Maybe she was right. Maybe by Tuesday evening she'd be yapping on the telephone with Tony instead of avoiding her. By that time, perhaps the only drama would be whether to wear matte lipstick or gloss.

Lacey found herself craning her neck in the hallway for a glimpse of Rob. Her crush on David had definitely taken a nosedive. By the time pre-calculus was over and she was well into a lecture on *Huckleberry Finn,* Lacey felt downright skittish. Choir was next period, and Rob would be there. But so would David.

Tony's eyes were bright with excitement when Lacey hurried into the music room.

"You will never guess what happened," she said to Lacey, dipping her head back slightly so that Lacey would know she was talking about David. "This will cheer you up."

"What?" Lacey said tersely. She could hear the rumble of David's voice as he boasted about a midnight motorcycle ride he'd taken with his cousin. She switched allegiance and stood on tiptoe, scanning the rows for a glimpse of Rob until she found his face. His eyes were trained on her. Lacey blushed and gave him a small Queen of England wave, vaguely aware that Tony was tapping her hard on the shoulder with the gleaming tip of her black-nailed finger.

"Are you listening to me?" Tony's harsh whisper tickled Lacey's earlobe. "It's important!"

Lacey gave Tony an oh-this-is-so-much-fun-and-don't-I-look-vivacious smile for the benefit of anyone who might be watching, pretending to be wildly interested in whatever her friend was telling her.

"What's so important?" she said brightly.

"Shhh!" Tony glanced behind her. David and Scott were intent on pummeling each other, and she continued, with a nod behind her. "They want us to go bowling with them on Friday."

It took Lacey a moment to register the information. "David?" she whispered in Tony's ear. "The David who's still avoiding me in the hallway?"

Tony chucked her chin up and down in rapid succession. "The very one," she said in a voice so low that Lacey had to lean her head on Tony's shoulder. "Scott said that David told him to tell me to ask you."

"Say that three times fast," mumbled Lacey, her eyes straying in Rob's direction again. "I don't know," she trailed off. "I suck at bowling."

"I thought you still liked him a little bit," Tony said in a voice that was close to pleading. She pulled sheets of music out of a folder, adding edgily, "If you're not interested anymore, I don't want to force you to go."

But you want me to, don't you? thought Lacey. It was odd discovering that smart, savvy Tony was as human as everybody else. She dressed the way she felt like dressing, she counseled Lacey not to date Charles Pincer or drink coffee if she detested it, and yet here she was asking Lacey to do something she didn't really want to do. But when push came to shove, Lacey would do what she could, just because Tony needed her. Even if it meant spending time with someone whose charm was fading fast.

"I guess I could see what David's like when he's not drunk," Lacey said softly.

"Or I can ask Caroline to go," said Tony, but her eyes were so bright and grateful that Lacey shook her head.

"Do you think my mother's boyfriend has a bowling shirt?" said Lacey, waiting expectantly for Tony's trill of laughter as she picked up her music folder.

Mr. Lenney tapped his baton on the music stand. *"Carmina Burana,"* he barked. "Rosie, get ready for your solo."

Lacey felt a surge in her heart as she sifted through her sheet music. She had loved to sing ever since she was a baby, but Rosie was the natural talent. Lacey couldn't help being proud of her sister, who had sung the solo in every school concert for as long as she could remember.

Something hard was pressing into her back and Lacey twisted around in her seat. David was kneeing her playfully. He mouthed the word "bowling" at her, drew a huge question mark in the air with his finger, and clasped his hands together in prayer.

Maybe he's not so bad, thought Lacey, shaking her head "yes" just as Mr. Lenney called out, "From the beginning."

Lacey inhaled deeply and readied herself to sing. Perhaps that's what she should do. Start at the beginning. David thumped her once more in the back as she sang the first note. In the second row of the bass section, she could see Rob bobbing his head ever so slightly in time to the music.

After school, Lacey hung around the house waiting for Rosie to come home. The couch had dried, and except for a small discolored patch of jade green, no one would ever have known that the sofa had been Sherman's sickbed.

Sherman was another matter. Lacey had called her mother at work, only to find that Leonora had left a few minutes earlier. Lacey poured herself a glass of orange juice and piled a handful of low-fat tortilla chips onto a napkin. Then she pulled a stack of books out of her knapsack and settled down to do her homework.

Lacey was in the middle of a math worksheet when she heard the front door open, then the clunk of metal hitting slate and the door slamming shut. There were swift, running steps up the stairs, followed by the patter of shoes along the hallway above her. A person of energy, a task completed. It had to be Leonora.

"Ma?" called Lacey, pausing to listen for an answer. She could hear water running now. Shrugging her shoulders, Lacey returned to her worksheet.

A few minutes later, the front door clicked open once more and closed gently. A second set of footsteps, slower and more tentative, mounted the stairs. It had to be Rosie.

Lacey left her schoolwork on the kitchen table and wound her way through the dining room and into the hallway. The cat carrier stood empty on the slate floor. She reached down and patted it until the tinny metal made a clanging sound, then trudged upstairs, hesitating at the top. A left turn would take her to her mother's bedroom, a right turn to Rosie's. Leonora first—maybe Rosie needed to be alone. She turned and met her mother head-on in the hallway.

"So?" she said softly. "How's Sherman?"

"It's done," said Leonora. "She was so old, Lacey, and so sick. Dr. Hamen said that she might have lived a few more months in terrible pain and then . . ."

"I don't understand," said Lacey, stiffening at the look on her mother's face.

"I had her put to sleep," said Leonora.

"You what?" said Lacey, raising her hands helplessly, pointlessly, in the air. She gripped her temples with spread fingertips and pitched her voice hysterically higher. "You had her *killed?*" she said hoarsely. "You *killed* her?"

"What are you saying?" Rosie stood next to her, her face the color of chalk dust.

"She *killed* her!" Lacey said to Rosie, and then again to Leonora, her voice agonizingly shrill.

Rosie pressed against the wall, dull eyes trained on Lacey's howling mouth. "How can you say that?" she cried. "You promised, Lacey! You know how hard this is for me! You promised to keep it a secret, and now the doctor says I can't even have it yet because I'm too anemic. I can't do anything, Lacey, even if I wanted to! And it's not a baby yet, you said so yourself!" Rosie's eyes, brimming with accusation, shifted from Lacey to Leonora. Her mother was a still snapshot, arms up in protest, mouth gaping.

"A what?" Leonora worked her tongue gingerly in her

mouth as if she had a canker sore. "Son of a bitch, Rosie. It's not a *what?*"

Rosie slid down the wall and tucked her head into her knees. Lacey slid limply next to her sister, assuming the same position. Her voice shook. "I was talking about Sherman," she said.

Rosie gave herself a ferocious hug now, wrapping her arms around her knees so tight that Lacey thought she might topple over. She improvised a rhythmic rocking motion, back and forth, like some mad creature in a gothic movie, Mr. Rochester's wife in *Jane Eyre* perhaps, raving in her padlocked room.

"I wasn't talking about you," Lacey persisted, putting the palm of her hand on Rosie's back to still her sister. "I was talking about Sherman."

"Sherman?" Rosie spoke to her knees.

"Sherman," said Lacey. "She was sick all over the sofa and Mom had her put to sleep."

Leonora sighed deeply as she lowered her body to the floor. The muscles around her mouth twitched as she struggled to get the words out. "Tell me it isn't so, girls. Oh my God, Rosie, please tell me you're not pregnant."

Lacey sprang to her feet like a cheerleader gone berserk, shouting, "No, Ma, we're not going to talk about Rosie now, we're going to talk about Sherman! Why did you have to kill her? Why couldn't you let her live just a little bit longer? What's the matter, she was ruining your new couch and your precious plans? Or did you have to get rid of the last good thing that belonged to Daddy?"

She was surprised to find herself panting now, like an exhausted runner who had crossed the finish line.

Leonora sucked in air and released it slowly, her own tortured brand of yogic cleansing breath. "She had cancer, Lacey. I saw no reason to prolong her pain. Don't you remember telling me that she was hiding in strange places? She was hiding in strange places to get away from the pain."

Rosie lifted her head an inch or two and murmured, "That's what I'd like to do."

"What, Rosie?" her mother said flatly, nostrils flaring. "What the hell would you like to do?"

"Stop cursing," Lacey murmured.

"It's in my nature," said Leonora without skipping a beat.

"You sound so mean," whispered Lacey, knowing full well that her own words had been a form of target practice.

Leonora shifted on the floor, shrugging her shoulders as she assumed the mantle of some new personality. "Do tell me, Rose," she addressed her daughter politely. "What is it you'd like to do?"

Rosie pressed her hand across her mouth. "Hide like Sherman to get away from the pain," she said through her fingers.

"Don't call her Rose," Lacey said fiercely. "She's not a Rose."

"She's a Rose on her birth certificate," said Leonora. "She's a Rose if she's pregnant."

"I am," said Rosie, sobbing.

"She is," said Lacey, starting to cry herself.

Leonora grunted as she pushed herself up from the floor. She arched her back and stuck out her chest as though she were readying herself for some beauty-pageant runway. Then she floated down the hallway, one hand skimming the small mound of her stomach. "The last thing you can do is hide," she said before she walked into the bedroom and shut the door.

12

♥

Leonora did not emerge from her bedroom until well after seven o'clock that evening. Eyes red and hooded, she entered the kitchen like someone sleep-walking, making no eye contact at all with Lacey or Rosie. The girls uttered faint "hello"s and continued eat-ing their scrambled eggs and toast.

If Leonora had taken no notice of her daughters, she had observed their food. "High cholesterol runs in the family" was the comment that echoed within the walls of the refrigerator as she removed a carton of leftover Chi-nese food from a shelf. She proceeded to hold the open container above a plate until a box-shaped portion of lo mein landed in its middle. Then she stuck the unappetiz-ing mound of food into the microwave, jabbing a few buttons until the whirring of the oven began. "Of course, this lo mein is probably swimming in the wrong kind of oil," she said, addressing no one in particular.

Lacey quickly discerned her mother's aversion to conversation about anything living. Cholesterol and lo mein could not hurt Leonora's psyche. Pregnancy could. She took a chance and changed the subject.

"We're going to Dad's this weekend," she told her, half hoping that the news of their departure would give her mother some comfort.

"Is he picking you up?"

Lacey nodded.

"So. You'll get to see the new baby," Leonora said icily. "Your new half sister."

"Chelsea Petra Levine."

"Lord give me strength."

"Petra is Ellie's grandmother's name."

"Just lovely," said Leonora, removing the lo mein from the oven at the sound of the beeper and sitting opposite the two girls. "Visiting a newborn will give you a chance to look into the future, won't it, Rosie?"

"Are you *trying* to be cruel, Ma, or is it just something that comes naturally?" Rosie spoke for the first time.

"It comes naturally," said her mother, shading her eyes with her hand as if a beam of light were blinding her.

Rosie pushed back from the table and picked up a container of pills that was next to the toaster. "I have to take these for two weeks to build up my blood," she said, giving them a rattle before handing them to her mother. "I'm anemic. Then I can have the abortion."

"How very nice for you." Leonora pried the cap off the bottle. "Look at the size of them," she said in a voice that was empty of emotion. "They look like horse pills.

I can remember taking vitamins this big when I was pregnant with you." She fastened her eyes on Rosie's stomach. "At least you aren't too far along. You're not, are you?"

"She'll still be under ten weeks," Lacey volunteered. "They don't want her over ten weeks."

"I see." Leonora was quiet. She stabbed a clump of lo mein with her fork and twirled it around and around before putting it in her mouth. It looked as though she were chewing glass. "You seem to be very well informed," she said to Lacey.

"She's been great," Rosie said hurriedly. "She went with me to the clinic the first time."

"Joseph went with her the second time," said Lacey, surprised and grateful that Rosie had appreciated her.

"And I suppose your mother will go with you the third time," said Leonora.

"You don't have to." Rosie grabbed the pill bottle from her mother and threw it carelessly onto the kitchen counter. It clattered into the sink.

"I hope the sink isn't full of water," Leonora said quietly.

"It's not," Rosie snarled, flopping down in her chair with such force that her mother looked with alarm at Rosie's belly.

Leonora composed herself and chose her words carefully. "Perhaps you should ask your father to go with you. Perhaps it would enlighten him to see how the family dynamics have developed, Rosie. His daughter pregnant around the same time that he has a new baby. Think about it. Your half sister could have been good friends with his grandchild. What fun."

Rosie's eyes filled with tears, and Lacey couldn't hold back any longer. "Why are you acting this way, Ma?" she said. "You're torturing her!"

Leonora rose from the table and flipped open the lid of the garbage can. She scraped the mound of noodles into the trash, murmuring, "What a waste."

"The lo mein, or my life?" Rosie's voice trembled.

Leonora held out her hands, pale wrists to the ceiling. "My disappointment is so great, Rosie, that it's . . ." She clasped her hands together as if she were about to pray, searching for the right word. "It's palpable," she said at last. "I could cut it with a knife. Chew it up and spit it out."

"How many times do I have to say I'm sorry?" said Rosie.

"Sorry won't do it." Leonora reached for the pot that she used for boiling water. "Would anyone like some tea?"

"Tea won't do it," said Rosie, shaking her head fiercely.

"It won't," said Lacey, but she lightened her tone. Her mother drank tea only when her stomach hurt, and judging by her face, it hurt a lot. Lacey took a deep breath and said in a small voice, "Hot chocolate might help."

"Hot chocolate?" Leonora hesitated. "Do you want some, too, Rosie?"

"With marshmallows?" Rosie's voice was so mournful that Lacey thought she saw her mother's eyes get misty.

"I don't think I have any marshmallows," said Leonora, gazing at Rosie's round flushed face. "You've loved marshmallows since you were a little girl." Her voice was foggy.

She turned abruptly away and stood on tiptoe, pulling jars and bottles and boxes out of the top cupboard with desperate abandon. "Where the hell are they?" she muttered as a tower of boxed macaroni, brown sugar, bow ties, couscous, granola, raisin bran, oatmeal, and ziti threatened to topple.

"It's not that important," said Rosie, but her mother dug farther in the back of the closet, stacking more piles, until the girls heard her shout, "Eureka!"

"Nobody uses that word in this century, Ma," said Lacey.

"They would if they'd found a box of Mallomars in a cupboard full of health food like I just did," said Leonora, beaming as she unwrapped the box and folded the flap back to reveal a dozen perfectly round chocolate mounds inside. "Here, Rosie," she said, holding the cookies under her older daughter's nose. "They have marshmallows in them."

Rosie took one, grinning. "They look like chocolate breasts," she said, "with little chocolate nipples, only smaller."

"Speak for yourself," said Lacey, taking a bite out of a cookie of her own. "They're bigger than mine are."

"Mine, too," said Leonora, sniffing at a cookie. "Mmm, don't they smell divine? I'm having one."

"It's after six," Lacey said in mock horror, "and you are actually eating a cookie, Mother?"

"The hell with it," said Leonora, biting into the soft white center. "Sometimes you just have to treat yourself."

The three of them consumed the entire box of cookies, downing glasses of skim milk after Leonora reminded them that osteoporosis ran in the family.

Lacey drained the last drop of milk from her glass and stood to clear the dishes. She waltzed over to the sink in a series of ballroom steps gone wrong, but the lightness felt right because the secret was out, was no longer hers alone. Lacey ran a stream of warm water over a china plate from Tiffany's that Grandma Pearl had given her mother on Lacey's birth. It had a matching mug with Beatrix Potter bunnies on it, and when the cup had broken a few years back, Lacey was shocked to see tears in her father's eyes. "He's such a softy," her mother had said as he gathered up the remains. The mug still sat in pieces in a bowl on the kitchen windowsill where her father had left it. "Aren't you going to throw it out?" Lacey asked her mother when Michael Levine had gone. But Leonora didn't have the heart.

Lacey placed the bunny plate carefully in the dish drainer and turned to see if there were any more dishes to clear. She gasped out loud, an involuntary act as she caught a glimpse of Sherman's dish sitting empty on the floor.

"What?" said Leonora in a voice that implied *I will not survive the smallest whiff of one more trauma.*

"Sherman," said Lacey, the lightness gone. She turned back toward the sink, but the trembling of her shoulders gave her away.

"Come here, honey," said Leonora, holding out her arms.

Lacey shook her head and stayed, a fixture by the sink. Her hands shielded her eyes like blinders as she sobbed in silence.

"Come to Mommy, sweetheart," Leonora insisted, until Lacey's shoulders softened and her arms fell to her sides. She sat on her mother's lap, crying into the crease of Leonora's neck, which smelled faintly of perfume. Her mother rocked her and Rosie leaned toward them, resting a cheek on Lacey's back until her sister's sobs subsided.

"My little women," Leonora said softly. Lacey lifted her head so that she could look into her mother's eyes, but there was no trace of cynicism as her mother murmured, "I always loved that book." She looked pointedly at Lacey. "Did you know that I wanted to call you Louisa? After Louisa May Alcott. Then Daddy came up with Lacey, and it was so sweet that I didn't have the heart to talk him out of it. But I wanted Louisa, and Lacey Louisa Levine sounded just awful. I wanted the love they had, I wanted the family. Do you know what I mean, girls?"

"The father was away," said Rosie.

"But he came back," said Lacey.

"He did." Leonora's voice was wistful. She shifted in her seat, rearranging her daughter's limbs as if she were an oversized rag doll.

"I must weigh a ton," said Lacey. Rosie chimed in with "All those fattening Mallomars!" which set off Leonora, who burst into laughter, and even Rosie laughed.

It was funny how the tears and the laughter cleared the air, although Rosie was still pregnant, Leonora was still horrified, and Sherman was still dead. Lacey slipped off her mother's lap and slumped, exhausted, into a kitchen chair. They sat companionably and began chatting about the weekend. Leonora and Vinnie had tickets to a show that his cousin was performing in, the girls would see their father, Rosie could bring her term paper with her and Lacey her math, because Michael Levine was better at it. Lacey waited for her mother to bring up the abortion, to question Rosie's decision, but Leonora took her time. At last, her back to the girls as she sprinkled cleanser in the sink, Leonora said, "You're okay with it, Rosie?"

Lacey watched her sister's eyelids flicker. There was a moment of silence before Rosie said, "Isn't it the only thing I can do, Ma?"

Leonora reached for the scouring pad. "I guess it is," she said softly. Then she began scrubbing the sink so vigorously that Lacey said, "You should put on your rubber gloves, Ma."

"Oh. I always forget and then it's too late." Leonora held out her reddened fingers. "Dishpan hands."

"Vinnie won't like it," Lacey blurted out, instantly sorry.

"Screw Vinnie," said her mother, laughing so loud that it reminded Lacey of the old I-can-live-without-a-man Leonora that she used to know.

"I'm going bowling on Friday," Lacey announced.

Executing a small pirouette, Leonora surprised her. She peered into her daughter's eyes and said, "Why so glum, little girl?"

"You can tell?" said Lacey, a catch in her throat as she

realized that her mother could still be a mother and read between the lines. "Should I really go bowling with Tony and Scott and David when I think I like this guy Rob, who helped me with Jason in the apartment building?"

"Has this Rob fellow asked you out for Friday night?" said Leonora.

"Nooo," Lacey said hesitantly. "But I wish he would."

"Then give David a chance, and you can go out with Rob some other time," Leonora said brightly. "A bird in the hand is worth two in the bush."

Lacey couldn't help feeling disappointed, but she also had no urge to tell her mother about David's debut performance. "Do you think so, Ma?" she said in a low voice.

"I know so," said Leonora. "But you don't sound too happy about it, honey."

"I think she'd rather get Rob in the bushes than David," said Rosie.

"Rosie!" said Lacey, grinning widely before she added, "If bush stands for tush, I would."

"Lord help me," sputtered Leonora.

When the telephone rang on Tuesday night, Leonora picked it up. "Vinnie?" she said lightly. "Oh!" Leonora cupped her hand over the receiver, yelling, "Lacey! Telephone! It's a boy," so loud that Lacey wanted to drop through the floor.

"Who is it?" she hissed at her mother, grabbing the telephone before she could actually ask. "Hello?" she said tentatively as Leonora walked away.

"Lacey?" said a voice. "It's a boy. It's Rob."

"Rob?" said Lacey, laughing. "How are you?"

"I'm fine. I just wanted to see how you're doing. Since you got locked up."

"Oh, the lockup," said Lacey, giggling. "Hasn't anyone told you that you should use proper English?"

It was Rob's turn to laugh. "This cute babysitter I know told me once," he said. "Seriously, Lacey, you're all right?"

"Mr. Drew is going to let me know if he's going to ask me to babysit again, after my crime of the century."

"Say no if he does, and go out with me instead."

"I'd love to!" Lacey berated herself mildly for not keeping the excitement out of her voice. What was it the stupid rule book that sat beside cousin Claudia's bed had said about getting and keeping a man? Don't be too available. Oh well, thought Lacey, screw that one. Get off the phone quickly. She would get off in a minute. Don't accept a date after Wednesday. It was only Tuesday. She could say yes.

"I'll pick you up around seven-thirty, and we can go to a movie or something," said Rob.

Lacey's heart fluttered and sank. "I can't," she cried. "I forgot that I have to visit my father. He's had a new baby."

"Pretty nifty, your dad having a baby and all that."

"His new wife," said Lacey dejectedly.

"Then how about Friday?"

Lacey felt like moaning. "I can't go on Friday. I'm busy on Friday. I promised Tony I'd do something with her."

"Oh?" said Rob curiously. "What do you have to do with her?"

"Go bowling." She clamped her mouth shut. Don't say another word, she told herself. Don't ask me another question, she prayed.

"With who?" Rob persisted.

"With her and Scott and somebody else."

"Ohhhhh," Rob said knowingly. "I get the picture. With Scott and pretty-boy Potter? He's your bowling partner?"

"Not really," Lacey protested. "Can't we get together next week or something?"

"At the risk of sounding like Mr. Drew, we'll see. Enjoy your bowling, though."

Lacey hung up with such force that the 911 sticker fell off the telephone and fluttered to the floor. Everything had gone wrong. First she'd sounded too eager. Then she'd sounded unavailable. It was impossible to explain David. And it was Rob who had hung up first. Lacey uttered a slew of swearwords, sounding a lot like Leonora at her very worst. Why couldn't she have said no to Tony and yes to Rob? Why did her father have to go and have a baby, anyway?

Her mother stood in the doorway. "That was Rob the tushman, I take it?"

Lacey didn't crack a smile. "I had to turn him down twice. He's never going to call me again, and now I have to go bowling on Friday. I hate bowling."

"He'll call," said Leonora, turning to leave. "Just don't let anybody knock your pins down," she called over her shoulder. "Not until you're good and ready. Not until you're thirty."

"Don't be disgusting!" Lacey called after her. "And don't be paranoid!"

"Can you blame me?" Leonora's voice carried into the room.

"I'm going to swear off men," Lacey shouted at the top of her voice.

"Ha!" her mother barked at her.

"I am!" The telephone rang so shrilly that Lacey jumped in her seat. "Hello?" she said, not bothering to sit through the two rings that would show the caller that you weren't waiting by the phone.

"Is Lee there?" said a very deep, very masculine voice that definitely wasn't Rob's.

"It's for you, Lee," Lacey shouted. She watched her mother pick up the telephone and turn to butter. "I'm going to puke," she said out loud, but her mother grabbed her hand and kissed it before she could leave.

13

❣

Leonora's car squealed to a stop at the entranceway to the Twenty Thousand Leagues under the Sea bowling alley.

"Have a good time, girls," she called melodiously as Lacey and Tony scrambled out of the automobile. With a wave of her freshly painted French-tipped nails, she revved up the engine and was gone.

Lacey couldn't help grinning. "She drives our car like it's a Maserati or something."

"Attitude," said Tony. "Hot date?"

"Who knows," Lacey replied.

Tony held the door open for her friend. "It must be weird for you," she said.

"You don't know the half of it," said Lacey, wrinkling up her nose at the wave of stale smoky air that hit her.

"Three women in the house, going out with different people. Like a sorority or something."

"Hardly. More like a zoo."

"Even so. You and your mother are in the same boat. She knows what you're going through."

"When she's around, she knows." Lacey studied the dank interior of the bowling alley and sniffed again. "We must be standing near the smoking section," she said. "What a dump."

"Who said that?" said Tony. "One of those old-time movie stars that you and your father always liked." Tony took Lacey's arm and led her into the door marked LADIES.

"I'm surprised you remember," said Lacey, scanning the walls and discovering that the bathroom had no mirror. She crouched in front of the metal towel dispenser and fluffed out her hair. "What a dump!" she repeated, winking at Tony. "I'll have to ask my dad who said that."

Tony stooped next to Lacey and pursed her lips at the dispenser. "Your father used to make believe he was that guy in *Casablanca*. Humphrey Bogart. What was it he always said?"

Lacey pitched her voice lower and growled, " 'Of all the gin joints in all the world, she has to pick this one to walk into.' Something like that. He loved Ingrid Bergman in that movie. He used to tell me I looked like her. Nutty, huh?" Lacey smiled, but she remembered clearly the day he'd heard her say that she was the "plain Jane" of the family. "You look like Ingrid Bergman," he chided her, "only younger." Then he'd walked out of the room and returned with a coffee-table book on movie stars open to a picture of the actress. "Can you see how luminous she is? You have that quality, Lacey. An incandescence." When he'd gone, she looked up the two words in the dictionary. "Flooded with light." "Shining brilliantly." Odd descriptions, but not unpleasant. Would any other man besides her father notice?

They left the ladies' room and stood a respectable distance from the front entrance. Lacey recalled her cousin's rule book. It would never do to look overeager. Piece of cake, she thought. Apprehensive was more like it.

"Elegant decor," said Tony, examining the mural on the wall beside the bowling lanes. Big blobby fish in bold neon colors swam through a sea of aqua and ultramarine and turquoise. Bowling balls were suspended to look like bubbles rising up from their mouths.

"Who was their decorator?" said Lacey, laughing.

"My five-year-old nephew." Tony plopped down on a bench against the wall and patted the seat beside her. "Sit," she said.

Lacey sat and shifted a critical eye from painting to people. Several men and women wearing white shirts with "Castelano's Car Maintenance" emblazoned on their backs bowled earnestly in front of the seaweed on one side of the huge room. The women wore big hair and frosted lipstick, and the men sported potbellies that hung over their belts. High-pitched whistles and roars of approval filled the air whenever anyone bowled a strike.

"If I grow up and become one of them," said Lacey, "please shoot me."

"They're having fun," said Tony, giggling. "So where are Scott and David, the big bowling jocks?"

181

"Maybe they're not coming," said Lacey, glancing over at Tony to see if she'd detected the hopeful note in her voice.

Tony shot her a reproachful look. "My mother always says if you can't say yes to someone and be gracious, then say no."

"Oh. So I should have said no?" Lacey leaned against her friend.

Tony leaned back. "You know I'm glad you came." There was a glint in her eyes as she pressed against Lacey. "She locks herself out of the apartment and meets a guy with a cute butt, and suddenly she's in love. How was I supposed to know?" Tony leaned harder as Lacey erupted into laughter. "Why on earth wouldn't you want to go bowling with the boy who drunkenly mauled you at a Halloween party?"

"I'm not 'suddenly in love,' " said Lacey, grinning foolishly. "It's just that Rob is . . . he's more my type."

"If you say so," said Tony, pulling Lacey up from the bench. "Let's get our bowling shoes." She took off toward the desk marked "Shoe Rental," but not before throwing over her shoulder, "David was your type a month ago, you know."

"Call me fickle." Lacey sidled up to Tony and eyed the rows of faded blue bowling shoes. "You're going to make me put my feet in those smelly things?" Lacey held out a lock of hair and looped it under Tony's nose. "I already smell like a cigarette," she said accusingly. "Take a whiff."

Tony sniffed and made the motions of barfing into the shoe she was holding. "Can I help it if you have porous hair?" she said, fishing in her pocketbook and handing Lacey a small atomizer. "Use this, you royal pain in the butt."

"I am, aren't I?" Lacey said, squinting at the label. "Musk?" She held the perfume six inches from her hair and spritzed.

"What size shoe?" the man behind the counter mumbled through lips that barely moved.

"Eight and a half," said Lacey, looking down at Tony's feet to see how big they were.

"Seven." Tony raised an eyebrow at Lacey. "Never knew I'd be bowling with Bigfoot," she teased. "Have you ever seen my mother's feet? They're enormous. She told me they went up two sizes when she was pregnant with me."

Lacey bent to slip off her shoes. "Remind me not to get pregnant," she said, her heart leaping at the word.

"I see Scott and David." Tony's mouth was as immobile as the shoe-rental man's.

"Tell me David's not wearing those horrible green pants."

"He's not."

"Tell me I smell good."

"You smell good."

"Tell me why I'm nervous."

"Because a part of you still likes him."

"Is that so?"

"That's so," said Tony. "I'm your best friend and I know these things." Her voice became higher and sweeter as she called out, "Hey, Scott, David! Over here!"

The two boys said "Hey" with the same degree of calculated indifference. Lacey noted it. Perhaps there was a rule book for boys that said, "Show no enthusiasm when greeting the girls you're supposed to like."

David ambled next to Lacey and delivered her an equally disinterested "What's going on?"

"Not much," said Lacey. "We got our shoes."

"Screw that," said David. He stuck out a sneakered foot. "I'm wearing these."

"Lane 6," Tony announced, beckoning for them all to follow.

Scott sat down behind a small computer and pressed some buttons. Tony's name appeared on the screen, then his own, followed by David's. "How do you spell 'Lacey'?" he said to her.

"Put down 'straitlaced,' " said David before she could say a word. "That'll do."

"I beg your pardon?" said Lacey, jabbing him with an elbow. "I am not!"

"She is not!" Tony piped up.

"Whatever," said David. "I know what I know."

"Maybe it's only with you," Lacey said boldly, aware of a sense of fearlessness that she hadn't felt before with him.

Scott and Tony hooted with laughter while David busied himself testing bowling balls.

"That's not what you told me," said Scott, putting his face in front of David's.

Lacey watched him blush from his chin to his forehead and went in for the kill. "Haven't you heard? David's best subject is English."

"It is?" said David, dumbfounded.

"He makes up great fiction," said Lacey, sticking a thumb and two fingers into the holes of a pink marbleized bowling ball. She lifted it into the air and tested its weight. "This one kind of reminds me of you. A lightweight."

"You go, girl," said Tony, joining Scott in another round of laughter at David's expense.

"Isn't it your turn to bowl?" David said gruffly.

Tony sprang to her feet and positioned her fingers in Lacey's pink bowling ball. "You don't mind if I steal your ball, do you, Lace?"

"What's mine is yours," said Lacey, smiling as Tony darted a few steps forward, hips twitching. Tony gave her right arm a forward swing and let the ball spin out of her hand. Every pin went down.

Tony jumped in the air, hopping along the wooden floor until she fell into Scott's outstretched arms. Lacey couldn't remember when Tony had looked prettier. She beamed as brightly as Leonora did whenever Vinnie Rizzo was mentioned, with a glow that warmed the cheeks and mouth and eyes. It occurred to Lacey that love made people luminous.

It was David's turn to bowl. Lacey watched his body spring into action and found herself comparing him with Rob. He was squarer and more compact, and his movements were brisker as he bowled himself a spare. She knew at that moment, as if all the pins had gone down in her head, that she would never beam at David the way Tony beamed at Scott. And he would never in a million years find her luminous.

But David had no idea. He ambled back onto the car-

185

pet and slung an arm around Lacey, nuzzling her neck. "What's that smell?" he said, screwing up his nose. "Eau de skunk?"

"It's musk," said Lacey, aware that she wasn't as stung as she might have been just a month before.

"Beats B.O.," said Tony, her champion. "When was the last time you showered, David?"

Lacey stood up and grabbed her pink bowling ball. She breathed in lungfuls of stale air and darted purposefully down the lane, eyes trained on the triangle of pins.

"Don't forget to let go of it," David called as the ball went flying.

"You're not supposed to talk when someone is bowling, are you?" Lacey watched the ball spin swiftly along the gutter and disappear. It was fitting. There was nothing here for her on this particular evening at this particular bowling alley, and Lacey knew it. She felt as free as a bird.

Perhaps her face revealed this, because when she sat down next to David he leaned toward her and said, "No hard feelings, are there?"

"About what?" Lacey gave him a dazzling smile.

David shifted uncomfortably in his seat. "About the Halloween party and everything. I was just kidding before, you know."

Lacey gazed at him, her lips curved and full, her eyes bright. She didn't say a word.

"You can't blame a guy for trying," he continued, then jumped to his feet as Scott bowled a strike. "Way to go!" he yelled.

"Way to go," said Lacey, glancing at the clock and wondering when it would be polite to go home.

When they left the bowling alley, Tony took Lacey aside.

"Are you having a good time?" she asked anxiously. "I'm beginning to feel guilty."

"For what?"

"Because I dragged you here, and David is beginning to score more points in the jerk category."

"As long as I never let him score points in any other area," said Lacey, "I can deal with him."

"And you won't hate me forever?" said Tony, searching Lacey's face for any sign of discomfort as if she were a physician inquiring about pain.

"I needed this," Lacey said emphatically. "Everything is very clear to me now."

"He doesn't do it for you anymore, does he?" said Tony, pricking up her head as Scott called her name.

"Scott wants you," said Lacey, slinging an arm around Tony. "But his friend's jerk quota is way too high."

A neighbor of Scott's offered to give them a ride into town. Lacey slid into the front seat, leaving David, Scott, and Tony to clamber behind her. She gave herself a mental pat on the back. No chance for any touchy-feely alone in the front seat. No chance for anything that she would regret.

Walking down Glen Street was another matter. Scott had gathered courage and looped an arm around Tony. She looped an arm back, so that their arms made partial pretzels. David the copycat quickly followed suit, but despite her newfound freedom, Lacey couldn't actually bring herself to shrug off his arm. She scrunched up her neck in a symbolic gesture, bracing herself to say something that would reject him forever in the kindest possible way. They sauntered down Glen Street, two by two, as she rehearsed a bunch of words in her head.

"I'm thirsty," said Scott, breaking away from the foursome and propelling Tony to the other side of the street. "Let's get a Coke or something."

Lacey watched in horror as Scott and Tony headed in the direction of the deli. She heard herself stammer, "I don't think I want anything."

David leaned heavily on her, guiding the two of them through local traffic until they reached the sidewalk. "Keep me company," he said to her. The door to the deli jingled open, its cheerful bells quickly transformed into somber chimes.

Lacey muttered a prayer to herself as they passed the glass display of prepared foods. She dragged her feet, slowed to a snail's pace, took tiny baby steps as the words "Don't let him be here, don't let me see his face behind the counter" echoed through her head. David reached behind him and, in a final death knell of a gesture, grabbed her hand.

Tony turned swiftly and gave Lacey a stricken look when Rob's baritone broke the silence.

"What can I get you guys?" he said, friendly enough until he caught sight of David's hand, gripping Lacey's. Lacey yanked her hand guiltily out of his and stuck it in

188

her pocket. She had done nothing wrong, just a small act of cowardice in not removing it sooner, but Rob's eyes had already rooted out the betrayal and were fastened on Scott, never straying for a moment from his face. Lacey felt like a child caught stealing a piece of bubblegum, except that bubblegum was sweet and tempting and David was not. She could hardly bring herself to look at Rob as he went about the business of serving his customers, putting Coke cans and straws and sacks of potato chips into a brown paper bag, and removing them compliantly when Scott said he didn't need a bag. Rob was vigilant in his narrow vision, and kept himself from giving Lacey so much as a second glance.

David spoke up. "Put a hamburger on the grill, will you?" But to his amazement, Rob shook his head.

"The grill is closed," he said as the door jingled open and another group of teenagers piled into the store.

"You're kidding," said David, but he shrugged his shoulders and handed Rob a buck for a bag of Cheez Doodles. Disappointment wasn't macho, Lacey decided as she trailed after the three others to the exit. She turned briefly and caught sight of Rob, peeling paper off a hamburger patty and tossing it onto the grill for the next customer. She heard the sizzle of grease as she walked out the door, and checked David's face to see if he'd noticed. He hadn't.

14

❣

When Michael Levine arrived on Saturday morning to collect his daughters, Leonora was waiting for him. Most days, Lacey's mother quietly absented herself to go food shopping or get a haircut or take a pair of pants to the cleaners when he was coming over. It didn't fool Lacey. Her mother still tended the open sore that was her missing husband, the kind some of the old people got in Aunt Fanny's nursing home, the kind that wouldn't heal. Lacey was familiar with the flicker of pain that lightning-charged her mother's pupils when she gazed at Michael Levine. His face was barely lined, his dark hair untouched by gray. He had the smooth boyish looks of a leaner Calvin Klein. Marrying Ellie had rejuvenated him further—divorce, in fact, was his fountain of youth.

Leonora was smiling at Michael now, possibly because he had pleased her by exclaiming, "Look how thin you've gotten, Lee. You look terrific!" Her dark mane, threaded with post-divorce white strands, had recently become a glossy burnished red color. Lacey felt some smugness about the change, which had been fueled by a comment she'd made to her mother. Would she, Lacey, go dark and grizzly like Grandma Pearl when she got older, or white like Leonora? She knew it had not been one of her finer remarks, but her mother had borne it quietly with an immediate purchase of Clairol's Loving Care that was put to use that very evening. "A woman of a certain age is supposed to go brighter or lighter," she told Lacey, opting for a brightening red that brought out her hazel eyes. "Aren't you glad I mentioned it?" Lacey asked her mother. Leonora responded by shaking her reddish mane in her daughter's face.

Despite a lack of wrinkles, Michael Levine wore the fatigued look of a new father, but his step was as energetic as ever. He strode cowboy-like and smiling into the living room after complimenting Leonora on her weight loss, but then took in her troubled expression. He knew his ex-wife well, and his smile faded.

"What's the matter?" he said, running his fingers through short spiky hair that was cut New York hip-style. It was a movement that was familiar to Lacey, a mark of her father's agitation. He'd done it when he fought hard with Leonora, he'd done it when Rosie had been his student driver and ran the car off the road instead of merging onto the highway. Lacey had watched silently from the back seat as her sister jammed on the brakes, her father scraping the fingers of his right hand through his hair. It was his "I am going to keep calm no matter what" gesture. He used it when Sherman had shattered his favorite coffee cup, and he began fingering his hair now as Leonora requested that they have a private discussion in the kitchen because she had something important to tell him.

"You can talk in front of me," Rosie said shrilly.

"No, we can't," said Leonora.

"Wait a minute, wait a minute. Is this about you, Rosie?" her father asked.

"It is," Leonora answered for her. "I thought it would be better if we talked alone first, Rosie."

Lacey felt the hairs on her arms prickle as a familiar combative tone crept into her father's voice. "If it's about Rosie, wouldn't it be smart to allow her to stay and listen?"

Leonora's posture sagged. She looked poised to reject Michael Levine's request but, to Lacey's surprise, pointed to the new sofa instead, saying, "Have it your way. Everybody please sit."

Lacey sat beside Rosie on the couch, the faded stain between her legs, as her mother held court.

"We have a bit of a family crisis here that I think you should know about," said Leonora. "I was tempted to tell you about it on the telephone, but thought that it would be better if we talked about it in person."

"I don't think it's a crisis anymore," said Rosie flatly. "I think the crisis is over."

"It's not as simple as that, Rosie." Leonora covered her mouth with her hand, then pulled it away. "Have I gone and smeared my lipstick now?" she said.

"Let's keep our priorities straight, Ma," Rosie said sarcastically. She addressed her father. "When you're ready to go, I'll be in my room." Then she stood up, stepping hard on Lacey's left foot, and trounced out of the room.

"Rosie!" cried Leonora. "I thought you wanted to be here!"

"Well, I don't!" Rosie's answer echoed from the stairwell.

"Will someone please tell me what's going on?" said Michael Levine.

"She's pregnant," announced Lacey. "When she finishes her pills for her anemia or whatever, she's going to get an abortion. That's why she thinks the crisis is over. We've come to a decision."

Leonora nodded at Lacey. "Did you notice the 'we'?" she said. "Her decision affects all of us, you know."

Michael Levine pressed back into his armchair. If he had been standing, he might have shuffled backward out of the room. "Rosie?" he said. "Rosie is pregnant?"

"Rosie. Our firstborn," said Leonora.

Lacey stiffened. Were they going to be treated to a barrage of snideness now?

"Didn't you talk to her?" A crease that had previously gone undetected appeared on Michael Levine's flawless forehead. "About birth control and, well, you know . . ."

"I didn't even know she was having sex," said Leonora. "But I had *soooo* much time for heart-to-heart talks, Michael, that I can't imagine how I could have been so remiss. I mean, just because I was working full-time and paying the bills and shuttling the girls around and trying to get the smallest amount of pleasure for myself. Silly me. How could I have forgotten to sit the girls down in the parlor before we did our embroidery and after we read our Emily Dickinson poetry? How could I have missed the opportunity to give them that talk about contraception?" Her voice was icy with contempt, nostrils flared into rigid ovals, fists clenched. The old Leonora was back, thought Lacey, and she hadn't been missed.

Leonora hadn't enjoyed her reemergence either. She closed her eyes for a few moments. Lacey watched as the frozen contours of her mother's face softened. "I'm sorry," she said at last. "I overreacted, Michael. I have a lot of guilt over all of this. Is it my fault that Rosie is pregnant? I hope not. I mean, who knows what the divorce did to the girls . . ." Her voice trailed off. "I don't know. Maybe it *is* my fault."

"It's nobody's fault," Michael Levine said emphatically. "I didn't mean it to come out that way."

"Okay." Leonora spoke softly.

"It was stupid of me to say that, Lee."

"Okay," Leonora repeated, her eyes welling up with tears. "Why the hell am I crying?"

Michael Levine smiled. "Maybe it's because we're actually talking to each other, Lee."

"You mean we're having a meaningful dialogue?" Leonora sighed. "You were probably right before. We should have discussed the pregnancy with Rosie right here. Your instincts were better than mine, Michael."

"They wrecked a few lives along the way."

Lacey spoke up. "I'm personally capable of wrecking my own life, Dad, without any of your help."

Leonora laughed. "You're not going to let us take credit for that, honey?"

Rosie appeared in the doorway. Lacey watched her father's eyes dart to her sister's stomach, then back to her face. "Is it over?" Rosie said. "Can we go now?"

"I don't know what to say, Rosie," said her father. "I'm sorry. Is that all right? For me to be sorry?"

"No," said Rosie. "Don't be sorry."

"If there's anything I can do, Rosie. I mean, is Joseph going to go with you, or your mother, or would you like me to go?"

"That would be downright weird," Lacey volunteered. "The father going with the daughter."

"Haven't you figured out yet that life is weird, Lacey?" said Leonora. "Your father has a new baby that I've never seen. That's kind of strange, isn't it?"

"Did you want to see the baby, Lee? I'm sorry!" Michael Levine looked confused.

"No, Michael. It's not that I'm dying to see the baby. I just wonder . . . Does she look like my children? Does she look like you?"

The mere mention of Chelsea Petra Levine switched on a light in Michael Levine's eyes. He said, "She looks so much like Rosie you wouldn't believe it. And she looked right at me, from birth, like Lacey did. It was unbelievable, Lee."

"Does Ellie know how much she looks like Rosie?"

"Hello!" Rosie interrupted. "Can we finish what we were talking about, please?"

"I'm sorry, honey," Leonora said hastily. "You've decided that you want Joseph to be there, haven't you?"

Rosie nodded. "Can we go now, please?"

Michael Levine and Leonora exchanged glances, in unspoken agreement that the matter hadn't been discussed as much as they would have liked. Lacey retrieved her knapsack from the hallway, and Rosie put on her coat in implicit agreement that the subject was closed.

The ride to Michael Levine's house was uneventful, except for an odd exchange when Lacey opened up the front door to the car and made the motion to sit down.

"The seat belt is broken in the back seat," protested Michael Levine. "I think Rosie should sit up front."

Rosie replied, "I don't care where I sit, Dad."

Lacey felt a flare of anger, but as she watched her father hesitate, it dawned on her.

Lacey climbed into the back seat, saying, "Don't you see, Rosie? He wants to protect you and the baby." The fact that Rosie's plans did not include keeping the baby did not seem to matter. Michael Levine felt bound to protect his grandchild-to-almost-be.

"Is that what I'm doing?" Michael Levine said sheepishly. "You're too smart for me, Lacey."

It was during lunch that Lacey told her father about Sherman. The look of sorrow in his eyes made her feel that he understood better than anyone what this loss meant to her. They ate at a diner in the local village, because Michael Levine didn't want his wife to feel that she had to feed them all. It was considerate of him, but Lacey had noticed many more considerations for Ellie Levine's comfort than had ever been afforded Leonora. For one thing, their father had always hated takeout food for dinner—and it seemed to be all they ate whenever they visited Michael and Ellie. And Michael Levine always ended the meal with, "That was great, Ellie. Wasn't it, girls?" When Lacey commented, "She didn't cook it," he looked daggers at her.

For another, the modern red-and-white kitchen, which was something Leonora had wanted all through their marriage but Michael Levine had said they couldn't afford. And the baby grand piano, which Michael Levine had given Ellie as a wedding present because she told him she had always wanted to play. It was too late for Rosie and Lacey to take lessons at home, but Ellie could. And so could their half sister.

Michael Levine headed straight for Chelsea the moment he entered the house. He took her from his wife's arms and bundled her into his own, kissing the top of her small fuzzy head with such tenderness that Lacey almost turned away.

"Come and meet your sisters," he crooned, holding her chubby cheek against his rougher one as he walked slowly toward Rosie and Lacey.

"Here she is." Michael Levine turned the baby toward Lacey. Her big brown eyes fastened themselves on Lacey with such alertness that she hardly seemed like a newborn.

"Can I hold her?" Lacey addressed Ellie, who stood off in a corner. "Would you like me to wash my hands, Ellie?"

Ellie shook her head and said, "Thank you for asking, Lacey. I must say, you're more considerate than some of my friends who come to visit me. They walk in here with the flu, for heaven's sake. Go ahead and hold her, honey."

"Careful of her neck," her father warned as she scooped up the baby. Chelsea rested against her shoulder while Lacey breathed in her half sister's scent. "She smells so good," she said, lifting the baby higher, with her right hand firmly against the baby's back.

"You're a natural," said her father.

"She is," said Ellie.

Lacey rocked the baby slowly, and turned toward her sister. "She does look like you, Rosie. She's got your coloring!" It dawned on Lacey that this piece of information might not sit happily with Ellie, but Ellie beamed good-naturedly at the four of them as if she were the mother of them all.

"Would you like to hold her, Rosie?" Ellie darted forward, lifting the baby out of Lacey's arms and shifting her into Rosie's.

"She's so soft and warm!" said Rosie, pressing her nose into the chubby crease of the baby's neck.

Lacey watched the two of them, round-faced and glowing, looking like sisters for certain, or maybe even mother and child, as the baby's curls blended with Rosie's fairness.

Ellie startled them out of their reverie. "Let me take a picture!" she called to them, running into the next room for the camera. She arranged the four of them on the couch, Michael Levine with his arm around Lacey, Lacey leaning against Rosie, and Rosie holding her half sister between the two of them, smiling widely.

It was Rosie's idea to let her father and Ellie go out to dinner that evening.

"We can babysit," she told them. "You probably haven't been out alone since you had the baby, have you?"

Forever the good girl, thought Lacey, but she reminded her father, who looked more concerned than Ellie, that she had cared for Jason since he was a little baby.

"It will do you good," Lacey told them, "and I'm an old hand at changing diapers."

Ellie was flushed and happy, and looked like a smaller, younger version of Lacey's mother as she put on her makeup: cappuccino-colored lip gloss with a thin line of pencil, not the bright reds and plums that Leonora preferred. Ellie burst out of the bathroom and grabbed Michael Levine's arm. "Let's make our escape," she said, "before the girls change their mind!"

"You look pretty," he told her, immediately giving his daughters an anxious glance, as if he had committed the crime of the century by complimenting his new wife in front of them.

"Italian food and red wine!" announced Ellie, eyes shining, and Lacey could see in that instant why her father had liked her in the first place.

Ellie sat down to nurse the baby. "I'll just give her a little top-up," she said, motioning for the girls to sit next to her as she positioned Chelsea discreetly under her T-shirt. "There's not much of me to hide," she said ruefully. "I'm the size of a teenager." Eyeing Rosie, she added, "More Lacey than you, honey."

Michael Levine interrupted them, holding a bottle in the air. "I've made up some formula and it's in the refrigerator if you need it. She takes it from me, once a day."

"I haven't been able to figure out how to use the damned breast pump yet," said Ellie, frowning in mock despair. "I tried it the other day and it took me an hour to get half an inch."

Ellie chatted softly, asking Lacey about homework and parties and how much babysitters charged, and Rosie about Joseph and choir and college plans, until Chelsea's eyelids started drooping and she fell asleep. Ellie shifted the baby gently off her breast, and carried her into the bedroom.

She emerged a few moments later, jabbing her fist in the air and crying "Freedom!" Then she took a jacket out of the closet and grabbed hold of her husband's hand, pulling him toward the front door. "I hope the girls can have some peace while we escape!" she said, waving gaily goodbye as they hurried out the door and down the walkway.

The moment the front door clicked shut, Chelsea began to cry. Rosie was the first to reach the crib. She bent to lift the baby and rocked her sideways, but the baby squeezed her eyes into slits and turned up the volume until her face was flushed from the effort. She showed no signs of stopping.

"This isn't working," said Rosie, but she shook her head when Lacey held out her arms, with the words, "Let me give it a try." Rosie began a series of rocking experiments, lifting the infant high or rocking her low, swinging her back and forth metronome-style. The baby continued squalling until Rosie discovered a deep-knee jogging motion and the cries became less desperate.

"It's starting to work," whispered Rosie, executing a series of rhythmic knee bends for several minutes until the sobs turned to whimpers, an occasional whisper of a gulp, and finally the soft shallow breathing of a sleeping infant.

"Put her back in the crib," said Lacey.

Rosie carried Chelsea to the nursery, turned abruptly, and ended up on the sofa. "I don't want to give her up yet," she said. "Can we sit here for a while?"

Lacey agreed, and they sat companionably making idle chatter about Ellie's decorating skills, the small touches that worked, the clinkers that didn't.

"I'm hungry," said Lacey, heading for the kitchen to examine the contents of the refrigerator. She returned with two fudge pops, unwrapping one and placing it in Rosie's free left hand.

"Weight Watchers," said Lacey, taking a bite of her ice cream. "She diets just like Mom does."

Rosie laughed, glancing down at the baby to make sure that she hadn't disturbed her slumber. "Dad probably wouldn't know what to do with a woman who wasn't constantly on a diet," she said.

"Probably not." Lacey put out her hand and stroked the baby's head. "She's adorable, isn't she?"

Rosie nodded.

"It's hard to admit it," said Lacey, taking her hand away when the baby started to peep, "but Ellie is kind of nice."

Rosie rocked Chelsea back and forth until the noises stopped.

"Don't you think so?" whispered Lacey.

Rosie nodded once more, lowering her cheek so that it touched the baby.

Lacey leaned her head on her sister's shoulder. Rosie lifted her head and tilted it sideways so that it rested against Lacey.

"I have that *Little Women* feeling," said Lacey. "The kind that Mom was talking about the other day. Three sisters together. Cozy. Close."

Rosie raised an eyebrow. "We are not your typical family," she said, but she didn't move her head away.

"And we have to rule out Beth," Lacey said hastily. "No family deaths, please." Oh no, she thought, had she inadvertently reminded Rosie of the abortion? Lacey hurried on. "But I guess family is family. I mean, Dad's still our father, and Mom's still our mother. We have a few extras now, like a half sister. And a stepmother who isn't the witch I thought she'd be. You know?" Lacey sighed. "If only I hadn't messed up so bad with Rob."

Rosie's voice was kind. "Things will work out," she said. "You know he likes you, otherwise he wouldn't have been so mad."

"I guess you're right."

"Maybe when you get back, you can go and visit him in the store." The baby started peeping again, and Rosie rubbed her back in a circular motion.

Lacey watched her sister. Was mothering instinctive in every female? Or did the seed of a baby in her sister's stomach give her an edge somehow? "You're good with her," she said at last. "I didn't know what the heck I was doing when I started taking care of Jason."

"Dad says you're a natural. Besides," Rosie said simply, "she's my sister." She turned toward Lacey with eyes bright with tears. "Am I doing the right thing, do you think?"

"I just told you how great you are with her!" Lacey exclaimed, but the instant her sister bent lower to caress the baby, she knew that Rosie wasn't talking about child care.

"I could never give her up," said Rosie.

"You don't have to," said Lacey with a fierceness that surprised her. "It's a fetus you're getting rid of, not a baby."

"I know," said Rosie. "I know that's true. But look what it turns into. Something so *beautiful.*"

"Let me put her to bed," said Lacey, grasping the baby so firmly that Rosie couldn't stop her. Perhaps if she removed the baby from her sister's arms, she could remove the indecision and doubt and mourning from her eyes as well.

Lacey and Rosie were curled up on the couch when Ellie and their father got home. Their stepmother thanked them profusely and excused herself. "I'm falling

203

asleep on my feet," she told them. They could hear her brushing her teeth in the bathroom around the same time that Chelsea started to scream.

"I'll get her," called Michael Levine, bounding toward the nursery and returning to the living room with a swaddled baby and a bottle. "I always give her a nighttime feeding," he explained. "By this time, Ellie is usually exhausted." He settled himself between the two girls, holding the bottle higher than the baby, so that she didn't have to suck on air. Chelsea trained her eyes on her father's face, sucking contentedly as she grasped his index finger with her tiny fist. Rosie arranged the fingers of her sister's other hand around her thumb.

Lacey could hear the baby swallow. She rested a hand on top of her father's, the one held tight by his miniature daughter. "Did you give us a bottle at night?" she asked.

"I wish I could tell you I did," he answered quietly. The baby drank greedily, closing her eyes in a brief display of ecstasy, blinking them open to look at her father again.

"When I was just out of college," Michael Levine began, "I didn't have a clue what I wanted to do with my life. And then I found out that my mother was dying. She had ovarian cancer, and the doctor told us she didn't have much time left. I slept a lot. I just couldn't get it together, my mother wasting away in her bed, my dad all holloweyed. I spent a lot of time sleeping."

Lacey squeezed her father's hand as he spoke. Out of the corner of her eye, she could see his Adam's apple wobble up and down in the stream of words spoken so quietly that she had to strain to hear them.

Her father continued. "It was still dark outside when I woke up one morning. Maybe it wasn't even morning yet. My mother was sitting on the edge of my bed in the darkness. When she spoke . . ." Her father stopped, and Lacey could see his Adam's apple falter as he swallowed once, then twice. "I could hear the tears in her voice," he said. "And she told me that she was so sorry she wouldn't be around to see me get married and have a baby. I was very quiet, lying there and not saying a word, like I was sleeping. Then she said, 'I know what a good father you'd make.' And she got up and walked away."

"How soon after that did she die?" asked Lacey.

Her father shook his head. "I honestly can't remember," he said. "But I do remember, when I had you children, wanting to make her words come true. I wanted it with all my heart. You have a right to hate me, because somehow over the years it all went wrong. But I've made a vow to myself that I'll be a better father to her."

"We don't hate you," said Rosie.

"Maybe you've learned all the good stuff and the bad stuff from us, Dad," said Lacey. "Maybe you can just use the good stuff on Chelsea."

Michael Levine's voice was childlike. "So you forgive me?" he said.

"Lacey and I are feeling all warm and fuzzy today, Dad," said Rosie. "We call it our *Little Women* day and it means we'll forgive you everything."

"But we've ruled out Beth," Lacey said quickly, glancing at the baby. "Because the part about Beth is so sad."

Michael Levine smiled. "That's all right, then," he said.

· · ·

The baby woke them all early on Sunday morning, and Lacey and Rosie returned home after breakfast. As they were leaving, their stepmother kissed them soundly on each cheek.

"Having you here was like having a mini-vacation," Ellie told them. "You were wonderful with your sister, girls. Thank you so much for giving your father and me a breather."

Leonora was in her bathrobe drinking coffee with Grandma Pearl when they walked into the house. Michael Levine, trailing behind them, impulsively kissed his ex-mother-in-law on the head.

"Hello, dear," cried Grandma, standing up to give him a kiss of her own.

Leonora turned to Lacey. "Honey, before I forget, go call the Drews and let them know if you can babysit tonight. They telephoned a few minutes ago."

"They're lucky to have Lacey as a babysitter," her father said in a loud voice as she dialed the Drews' number.

Lacey shushed him when Bob Drew answered the phone. "Seven-thirty is fine," she said, resisting the temptation to tell her employer that it was big of him to trust her again.

"Looking good, Lee," Lacey heard her father remark, noting the old familiar twinkle in his eye.

Leonora pulled her robe closer to her. "Heavens, Michael," she said. "I haven't even brushed my teeth yet!"

"He's seen worse, haven't you?" said Grandma Pearl. "How are you, Michael?"

"He's a doting new father," said Leonora as graciously as she could.

"She's adorable," said Rosie.

"She is," Lacey agreed.

"You have wonderful children and wonderful grand-children," said Michael Levine. "They gave Ellie and me a break last night by babysitting for Chelsea. Ellie couldn't believe how great they were. Really, Lee. You done good."

Leonora smiled. "We did," she said. "Sit down and have some coffee before you drive back."

The five of them sat around the kitchen table, the girls extolling their new sister, Rosie describing her special rocking discovery that was guaranteed to put Chelsea to sleep.

Leonora started to laugh. "I used to rock the two of you like that," she said. "I read about it in the newspaper."

"She was so delicious I couldn't put her down," said Rosie.

"She wouldn't let me hold her at all," Lacey complained good-naturedly.

"Ellie's nursing," Rosie told them. "She's all bent out of shape because her boobs didn't really get any bigger."

"That's odd," said Grandma. "I went up a whole size when I was pregnant with your mother." She paused for a moment and barreled on. "You look like you might be getting a little bigger yourself, Rosie."

"Mom told you," said Rosie, her voice dipping.

"Don't be mad at your mother. I pried it out of her."

"It's okay." Rosie cleared her throat. "Because I have something I want to say to you all."

Leonora glanced at Michael, who began raking his fingers through his hair.

"What have you got to tell us?" said Lacey, more curious than fearful.

"Just let me get a cigarette," said Grandma Pearl, pushing back from the table.

Rosie held up a hand. "Grandma," she said. "Please don't."

"Don't?" said Grandma Pearl, but she straightened up in her chair like a chastised child and trained her eyes on her granddaughter.

"Are you ready?" said Rosie, drawing in a breath.

Grandma Pearl nodded. Leonora looked grim. Lacey and her father maintained neutral expressions.

Rosie's voice shook with a skewed vibrato. "I've decided not to go ahead with the abortion." She covered her mouth with her hands, as if she meant to censor herself, but the words were out already.

Leonora was the first to speak. "Does Joseph know about this?" she said.

"Joseph isn't the one making the decision," said Rosie. "I am. And I'm going to have the baby."

"What about school, Rosie? What about your future?"

Rosie's eyes grew glittery with tears. "I held Chelsea in my arms yesterday, and I rocked her, and she smelled so sweet, like baby powder, and I just don't think I can have an abortion, Ma. It's too hard." She shifted her gaze from Leonora to her father, from her father to her grandmother, from her grandmother to Lacey. "Lacey, help me," she said, pleading.

Lacey looked at her sister, trembling in her seat, with her hands on her belly now. "It's *her* baby," said Lacey.

The only sound in the kitchen was the clink of Grandma Pearl's coffee cup hitting the saucer. "Damn it!' she swore loudly. "I've gone and burnt my tongue."

Leonora groaned, sliding down in her chair. "Here we go again."

15

♥

Michael Levine spent the rest of the morning sequestered in the kitchen with Rosie, Leonora, and Grandma Pearl. Lacey wandered in and out, catching snatches of conversation as she did a load of laundry in the basement, finished up a book report in the dining room, and called Tony from the phone in the living room to see if she and Scott were still an item.

"We went out again on Saturday," gushed Tony. "I'm crazy about him."

"He seems crazy about you, too," said Lacey, flinching at a stab of envy that took her by surprise. She clamped down on it and made a vow that she would not be jealous of her best friend; she would simply not allow it. Lacey shifted the conversation closer to home, saying, "We have our own craziness going on here." Surely it was time to tell Tony about Rosie, who would be showing soon enough, no matter how oversized a designer T-shirt she wore.

"You'll never guess what's going on with my sister." After weeks of keeping quiet, Lacey felt a different kind of guilt tickle her conscience. Was she betraying Rosie by treating her secret as if it were a juicy new twist in the Levine daytime soap opera?

Tony was hooked. "Tell!" she said.

"Rosie is pregnant, and she wants to keep the baby and the family is in the kitchen trying to talk her out of it."

"Holy shit."

"That's sort of what my mother and grandmother just said. Hold on." Lacey held the receiver in the air for several seconds so that snatches of kitchen conversation might waft into the phone. "Can you hear them?"

"No. What are they saying?"

"Well. Grandma is telling her . . . jeez . . . Grandma is telling her that, back in the olden days, she had an abortion. An illegal one. That Rosie is lucky she can have a safe and healthy one now."

"What's Rosie saying?"

"Rosie doesn't care. Oh. Rosie is all gung-ho about the baby because we took care of my stepsister, who is the most adorable little thing in the world. And my mother is saying that she does not want to raise another child. That she will not support the baby. That she can't do it."

"And what's happening now?"

"Oh boy. I'd better get off the phone."

"Don't leave me hanging here, Lace!"

"No, really. My mother is upset. Very upset. I'll call you from the Drews'."

Lacey returned to the kitchen to find Grandma Pearl with her arm around Leonora, and her father with his arm around Rosie. Muffled sobs were coming from both sides of the table.

Grandma Pearl released her daughter and straightened up suddenly. "I saw something in the classifieds," she cried.

Leonora looked at her as if she were stark raving mad. "Mother," she said, shaking coffee-cake crumbs off a napkin and wiping her tear-stained face. "What on earth are you talking about?"

"Where the hell did I put my newspaper?" By this time, Grandma Pearl was rummaging through her handbag, which she abandoned several seconds later, contents scattered across the kitchen table, lipsticks and ballpoint pens rolling against coffee cups. Then she was flying out the front door, clutching her car keys.

Lacey followed, providing a narrative for the rest of the family. "She's searching the car now," she reported back to Rosie and her parents. "She's reading a newspaper."

"Here it is," Grandma called triumphantly, holding the newspaper under her nose as she walked back into the house. "In the classifieds section. Listen. 'Happily married couple, Florida-based, want very much to adopt newborn. You can be confident we will provide loving and secure home and excellent education. Medical/legal expenses paid. Please call Polly and Lance 1-800-841-8954. What do you think?"

"Have my baby and give her away?" Rosie said tearfully. "I just don't think I could do it." She hesitated. "What was the name of the woman? Polly? I could never give her to someone called Polly."

Lacey tried to be helpful. "Maybe they live near Disney World," she said. "She'd definitely get a tan."

"Tans are out," said Rosie. "Skin cancer, remember? And what kind of education can you get in Florida?" she said.

"The father's name is pretty lame, too. Lance?" Lacey made a face. "Don't you lance a boil or something?"

"What are you thinking, the both of you?" said Leonora, eyes flashing. "Rosie, we're talking about your future here! Names and tans don't matter, Lacey!"

Lacey's voice was icy. "This is the way teenagers think, Ma."

"And that's the very reason a teenager should not have a baby," said Leonora, blowing her nose on her napkin. "It's downright scary."

"You heard what Dad said," cried Rosie. "I took care of Chelsea just fine. And you're always telling me that I'm the responsible one in the family, aren't you?"

"Rosie," said her mother. "It's not like carrying around a sack of flour, the way they did in your school last year. I mean, it was a nice try, but it doesn't really teach you how hard it is. How tedious and backbreaking and . . . It's not only lugging and carrying. It's . . ." Leonora's voice shook.

Rosie interrupted. "You always told us that having children was the best thing you ever did, Ma. Was that just bullshit?"

"It wasn't just bullshit. I was in love with your father and I wanted to get married and . . ."

"You never even finished college, did you, Ma?" said Rosie.

"And you always said you'd go back," added Lacey.

"Mother." Leonora rested her cheek on the kitchen table. "Help me out here."

Grandma Pearl's voice rang out from her kitchen-chair pulpit. "The baby always comes first, Rose, not to mention food and clothing and diapers and doctors and staying up all night with a sick child and the stultifying boredom of caring for an infant and the sheer hard labor and being more tired than you've ever been in your life. With no job. No money. Joseph doesn't sound as though he's ready to be a father right now, does he? So think about it. No life. Period."

"Amen," breathed out Leonora.

Michael Levine's voice was calmer. "What about an open adoption, Rosie? Why don't we think about that?"

"What is it?" Rosie said miserably, dabbing at her eyes with the corner of her T-shirt.

Grandma Pearl jumped on the bandwagon. "Milton Shapiro, my lawyer, could help us, I'm sure."

"Just let me explain it to her, Pearl. It's where the child and the mother keep in touch with each other. They have some kind of relationship." A faint crease formed on Michael Levine's forehead. "That's why it's called 'open.' They used to keep the mother's name secret, which made it very hard for the child to ever find out who her parents were. This way, we could keep in touch from the start. What do you think about that?"

"Maybe Daddy has a good idea, Rosie," Leonora said faintly. "I went and visited the clinic, you know. They were very nice there. They told me about your options."

"Why did you do that?" Rosie's voice was harsh. "They just love to use that word 'options,' don't they? Like I said to myself, 'Gee, I think I'll screw up my life right now and get pregnant. Now, let's see what my options are.' Why the hell did you have to go there, Ma?"

"I wanted to make sure you were getting the best care, Rosie. It was all very confidential, and they wouldn't speak to me about your particular case. But they showed me around, and I got to ask the counselor a few questions."

Rosie sniffed. "What did you need to ask them?"

"We found out everything we needed to know," Lacey protested. "Believe me, Ma."

"I know, honey. I just wanted to check out the doctor's references and everything. I asked the counselor what most of the girls coming to the clinic do."

"What did she say, Lee?" said Michael Levine.

"She said, 'If they have plans in place, they usually have an abortion.' That's what she said."

"And if they don't?" said Grandma Pearl.

"If they don't, they keep the child."

"I have plans in place," Rosie said quietly. "So screw her little theory."

"Your plans could go on hold forever," said Grandma.

Lacey spoke up. "You're not going to like this, Rosie, but I have to ask. Do you think they'll let you sing the solo in the school concert if you're pregnant? And what about cheerleading?" She blanched at her own cruelty

215

the moment the words were out of her mouth. But she could see the picture so clearly . . . Rosie in a flower-sprigged dress singing a song about spring with her great big child-bearing belly sticking out. Spring had sprung in more ways than one. She would be the laughingstock of the assembly. And how about Rosie, rooting for the team, "Rah, rah," with a stomach as big as a watermelon?

Rosie started rubbing her eyes with her fists, crying, "Why is this happening to me?" She pushed back violently in her chair, rushing out of the room as the seat crashed backward onto the floor.

Michael Levine righted the chair. "We could have done without that, Lacey," he said.

Grandma Pearl banged on the kitchen table, her hand a gavel as she defended her granddaughter. "She was right to say it, don't you see? That's the way teenagers think, which is exactly why teenagers shouldn't be having babies. Our Rosie is so upset about not singing a song, when she should be worried about where she'll get the money to buy diapers and formula, and what it will be like, raising a child without a father."

"She'll be a mother while I'm still acting like a teenager," said Lacey.

"Her childhood will be over," said Grandma.

"Sweet heaven, I'm not ready to be a grandmother," said Leonora, rubbing her stomach. She glanced up at the kitchen clock. "When did we have breakfast, Ma? Could I be hungry already?"

"Nerves," said Grandma. "You're hungry because you're nervous."

"I wouldn't mind a sandwich or something," said Michael Levine.

Leonora stood up and peered in the refrigerator. "I haven't had a moment to shop," she said. "We have a head of lettuce, some tofu dogs, and tabbouleh salad."

"Any turkey for a sandwich?" Michael Levine said hopefully.

"No such luck," said Leonora, her voice so steeped in sadness that Michael reached out and took her hand.

"We'll work something out, Lee."

"I know," she whispered. "I just can't bring up another child, Michael. Can we talk some more about the open adoption with her?"

"After lunch?"

"After lunch. If we can't figure this out, I'm running away from home."

Running away from home sounded good to Lacey. It occurred to her that she could escape the kitchen and see Rob at the very same time. "How about if I go over to the deli and get some turkey and a few rolls," she volunteered.

"Would that be okay, Lee? I can take her in the car."

"It's fine with me," said Leonora.

"If you don't mind, Dad," Lacey said quickly, "I could use the exercise. By the time somebody sets the table and gets out the salad, I can jog there and back."

Nobody questioned the fact that they had never seen Lacey jog in her life. She raced down the street toward the deli and, before she'd rounded the first bend in the road, felt a sharp pain in her side. Pressing the spot with her fin-

217

gers, she sped on. "I will set things straight with Rob," she vowed, and as the throbbing continued, she made a second resolution. "I will begin a strict exercise regimen." Rob jogged. Maybe, someday in the future, they could jog together.

Lacey reached the flower shop and stopped, panting in front of the plate-glass window. She glanced at her reflection—she looked windswept and carefree, despite the crick in her side. There was no sign that she might be an aunt in less than a year.

Lacey opened the deli door to the usual jingle of bells. A fortuitous sound, she was sure of it. She walked briskly past the deli counter with the sign propped up on it, "Today's special: Pea Soup." She loved pea soup and so did her father. Perhaps she would get some. When she reached the cash register, Rob's boyish good looks were nowhere to be found. Jake stood there, wrinkled and leathery in a white cotton apron tied around his waist, a splash of green the color of peas across the front of it.

"What can I do for you, young lady?" he said.

"A pound of turkey and six kaiser rolls," Lacey said glumly; then she heard the familiar sound of Rob's voice coming from the back of the store. The sweet greeting she was ready to send him froze in the back of her throat at the sight of his arm resting lightly on blond half-pint Caroline's shoulder. The Caroline with the crystal-blue eyes that flickered, the Caroline who used to be her friend.

Lacey went through the motions of paying for her purchase and taking the bag that Jake held out to her. She pocketed the change to her brand-new mantra: *Don't look back, don't ever look back.* But it was as if she were living inside the Greek myth about Medusa, the monster with the snakes for hair who turned anyone into stone who looked at her—because she just couldn't help it, she had to see Rob one more time. Lacey moved her neck slightly, her pupils darting all the way to the right, but she was stone already, and Rob, the monster without any snakes, caught sight of her. His arm shot into the air, like a reflex response to a doctor's hammer on his elbow. Was it a wave or a reaction? Lacey didn't stop to find out as she bolted for the door, gripping the bag, calling "Bye!" much too loud over the sound of the jingling bells. She'd forgotten all about the pea soup.

16

♥

Lacey muttered hello to Grandma Pearl, who was sitting on the front steps smoking a cigarette, and slipped into the house, clutching the bag of rolls and roast turkey to her wounded heart. Rosie and her parents were seated in the living room, three dejected stooges way past the combative stage. No face-slapping here, no two fingers digging into eyeballs, not a single high-pitched whoop. A shroud-like peace had settled on them, which didn't stop Rosie and her mother from training their antennae on Lacey's gloomy face as she crossed in front of them.

"You went to the deli, Lace?" Rosie said, at the same time that her mother asked, "Is something wrong, honey?"

"Everything is hunky-dory." Lacey shot an aggrieved look at Rosie, who surely must have told her parents about Rob and the deli. She scurried past them into the kitchen, attacking the turkey wrapper as if it were Rob, crumpling it into a tight ball and tossing it straight in the garbage can. Then she slapped the turkey onto a plate, *Take that, Miss Flutter-face,* and laid a piece of paper towel inside a bread basket that was Caroline's head. She slam-dunked five rolls into the basket; the sixth skidded across the table and landed on the floor. Lacey retrieved it with a grimace, picking a long strand of hair off the bed of poppy seeds. "Too bad," she muttered, pursing her lips and blowing across its crusty surface before tossing it back in the bread basket. "Lunch!" she cried.

Leonora, Rosie, and her father filed solemnly through the kitchen door.

"I take it you saw him," said Rosie without skipping a beat.

"Saw who?" said Grandma, coming up behind Rosie. "What did I miss? I thought Lacey went to the super-market."

"Never mind, Ma," said Leonora. "Would you like us to leave, honey?" she said. "Do you want to talk to Rosie alone?"

"It's okay," said Lacey, unexpectedly grateful for the at-tention. She yanked open the utensil drawer and pulled out a bread knife. "I saw him all right," she said, shaking the knife dramatically in the air. "At the back of the store with his arm around Caroline."

Her father stepped forward as if on cue and gently wrested the knife from her grip. "I'll cut the rolls," he said.

221

Lacey sank dejectedly into a kitchen chair. "I'm not going to hurt myself if that's what you're thinking," she said.

"It's Caroline he's worried about," Rosie joked, sitting next to her sister and giving her arm a squeeze.

Leonora shifted the plate of turkey and the basket of rolls from the counter onto the kitchen table. "Who wants mustard and who wants mayonnaise?" she asked. "The seltzer is out on the table."

"Mustard," said her daughters.

"Mayo," said her ex-husband. "Is there any real soda?"

Grandma Pearl made a clucking noise of disapproval and Leonora chided him. "You're behind the times, Michael," she said. "We're watching our cholesterol and sugar and fat in this household."

"That's why you all look so healthy and beautiful," Michael Levine said gallantly.

Rosie patted her stomach. "I'm a regular picture of health," she said. "A teenage poster girl."

"And I'm so beautiful that Rob's with Caroline," said Lacey. "Maybe if I start blinking my eyes or something I can get his attention."

"I'm sorry," Rosie said. "I guess my idea for you to go and see him at the store kind of backfired."

"It might have worked out," said Lacey, plucking a roll from the basket. Her voice softened as she made the comment, "*You* seem a little better."

Rosie selected a roll of her own. "I'll survive," she said.

"And I'm not going to let the two of them ruin my appetite," said Lacey, piling roast turkey on her kaiser roll.

"That's the spirit," said Leonora. "Let Rob have that chick with the tic if he wants her!"

"Mother!" cried Lacey, turning away so that she could hide the broad smile that lit up her face.

Rosie said wickedly, "Yeah, that Rob is a dick if he picks a chick with a tic, don't you think?"

Her father slathered his roll with a mound of mayonnaise, singing, "He'll be sor-ry!"

"My Lacey is the cream of the crop," said Grandma Pearl, gesturing in the air with a tender lettuce leaf held between two fingers.

"Cream?" said Lacey in mock horror. "Much too much fat!"

"You have a beautiful figure," Grandma protested so loud that everyone started to laugh. Undeterred, she turned her attention on her daughter. "I thought you were hungry, Lee Lee."

"I promise I'll eat in a minute," said Leonora. "I'm just happy to have my family all around me."

Rosie put her sandwich aside and started to speak. Her voice sounded strange, but it was hard to tell if it was the turkey or tears or laughter. "I'm sorry for everything I've put you through," she said.

"We love you, honey," said her father. "We want to help you." He turned to address his second daughter. "I've told you this before, Lacey, but it bears repeating. Someone is out there who will appreciate your beauty, inside and out."

"Amen," said Leonora.

"Ma," said Rosie, "are you getting religious on us with all this 'amen' stuff we're hearing today?"

Leonora grinned. "I figure some days it's time to thank God for what we have. Today is one of them."

"Hey, Ma," said Lacey, suppressing a giggle. "Doesn't it feel like we're on one of those talk shows you used to watch, confessing all our problems and stuff?"

"Heaven forbid!" cried Leonora.

"Lucky me," Rosie said ruefully. "I'm the main attraction. The major geek who happens to be pregnant. May I have a drumroll, please, so I can let you know what I've decided to do?"

"Just tell us, darling," prompted Grandma.

Lacey took stock of the family as they leaned toward Rosie. Her mother's face was shiny with concern; her father's eyes were tender. Grandma stroked Rosie's hand with work-worn fingers wearing gaudy rings.

"I'm going to have the baby. And I want an open adoption."

Leonora stepped behind Rosie and wrapped her arms around her daughter. "Okay," she whispered in her ear. "Okay."

Lacey had no idea what prompted her, but she heard herself say, "Can we call her Louisa?"

"Louisa?" said Rosie. "Louisa." She tested the name out on her tongue. "Louisa May is kind of pretty, don't you think?"

"Maybe it will give her good luck," said Lacey. "She can have one of those *Little Women* lives that we were talking about, remember?"

"Forget about it," Rosie replied, her tone so sharp that Lacey's eyes widened in surprise. "Have you read the book lately?" she continued. "Jo is a wreck! She cuts off her hair to make some money and she leads poor Laurie on until she meets a randy old professor who tells her how to write! And Meg, for God's sake . . . what does Meg want? She wants the husband and the baby and the white picket fence, which is fine for some people, but how about a career? And what happens to the good girl? What happens to Beth? You've said it yourself, Lacey. She croaks. And Amy, the artistic one? Sure Amy gets the prize because Amy gets Laurie, but if you ask me, he was gay."

There was a stunned silence in the kitchen. Finally Grandma Pearl said, "I'm sure he wasn't."

Michael Levine cleared his throat. "But Katharine Hepburn was a feisty Jo, wasn't she? In the movie? And so was what's-her-name, in the remake." Rosie shot him a withering look and he added in a small voice, "Feistiness is good. Don't you think so, honey?"

"It's fine," said Rosie wearily. "But that's not what I mean."

"Louisa May doesn't have to be feisty or get married or write books or anything," Lacey said loudly. "She just has to be loved."

"That's right," said Rosie. "That's absolutely right."

"Love is good," Grandma said, patting Lacey's hand.

"Love is very good," echoed Leonora, with a glance at Michael.

"I just want everybody to be happy!" wailed Lacey. "Is that too much to ask?"

"No, it's not," said Grandma.

"I agree," chimed in Michael Levine, lifting his glass of seltzer high in the air. "I'll drink to happiness!" he cried, a stream of bubbly water sloshing over the side of the cup and running down his shirtsleeve.

"He's all wet," said Grandma Pearl. "Someone get him a paper towel."

"You're soaked," said Leonora, grinning as she wrapped the dish towel around his wet sleeve.

"See?" said Michael Levine. "See how everybody cares?"

"What a family," moaned Rosie. But a smile spread across her face which prompted Lacey to spring out of her chair, crying, "Happy, happy, happy!"

Rosie started laughing and Lacey joined her. Their father turned cheerleader, making "rah rah" noises with his hands in the air as the dish towel went sailing and landed on top of Grandma's coffee cup.

"Eat your lunch," said Grandma sternly.

"Yes, ma'am," said Michael Levine, settling back in his chair and taking an enormous bite of his overstuffed sandwich.

"Wait a minute," said Lacey.

"Now what?" said Leonora.

"What happens if it's a boy?"

All eyes turned to Rosie, who thought for a moment and said, "I'll just have to call him Louis then."

Grandma narrowed her eyes and examined her granddaughter. "Don't worry about it," she said with conviction. "It's a girl, for sure."

"How do you know?" said Rosie.

"A girl robs you of your beauty."

"Mother!" said Leonora. "That's an old wives' tale."

Grandma ignored her. "Now stand up and turn around," she said to Rosie.

Rosie did as she was told.

"It's a girl," Grandma Pearl repeated. "You're gonna be all butt, I can tell already."

"Thanks so much for sharing," Rosie replied.

Leonora pointed to her mother. "She made me what I am today, girls. Remember that."

Rosie spoke up. "What if they don't let me name the baby Louisa?"

"Grandma?" Lacey said anxiously.

"Maybe we can ask the lawyer to put it in the contract," Grandma said swiftly.

"Or, if that doesn't work," said Leonora, "she can be Louisa in our hearts, honey."

"Rosie," said Michael Levine, "don't rule out having a baby of your own someday. You could always call *her* Louisa."

"Michael!" cried Leonora. "Can we please just have this one first?" She fanned herself with her napkin. "I didn't mean for that to come out so nasty."

"I know you didn't, Lee," said Michael.

Lacey looked from her grandmother to Leonora, from Leonora to Rosie. So Rosie had decided. Someday she *would* be holding a little girl in her arms, a little girl that she would give away. Louisa May. Would she be a "good girl" like Rosie, and sing like an angel? Would she be big-busted like her mother or large in the hips like Leonora and Lacey? Would she read at four years old? Or would her adoptive family mold and change her without even knowing it, until the genetic part was but an underpinning on which a new mother and father and home would build up her character and personality? But Lacey's mother had always told her that she was "Lacey" at birth. That she already had her own personality, and so did Rosie. It gave Lacey some comfort. Louisa would always be theirs, in some part. She would not be able to shrug them off so easily. They would lose her to another family, that much was certain. And they might not be the first to see her walk. Or laugh. Or write her own name in crooked letters. But they would not lose her completely. And she would not lose them.

"Eat up," said Grandma. "You're eating for two now, Rosie."

"Three if you count my butt," said Rosie.

"Amen," said Lacey, and they ate their lunch.

Jason gave Lacey a hug that nearly knocked her over.

"He keeps saying he wants to get locked up again," said Mrs. Drew, looking lovingly at the little boy, who was close to strangling the babysitter crouched on the floor in front of him.

Lacey disengaged herself, saying, "We had an adventure, didn't we, Jase?"

"Let's go see Rob again. Let's get locked up!"

"Locked out," his father corrected as he came into the room. "Lacey won't be leaving the apartment again without her keys, will you, Lacey?"

"No, sir," said Lacey, too full of goodwill to get angry. "We'll have an adventure inside the house, Jason."

"We can watch *The Wizard of Oz!*" said the little boy. "You can be Dorothy and I can be the Scarecrow."

"You've been watching that show all week, Jason," said his mother. "I have 'Somewhere Over the Rainbow' coming out of my ears! Now kiss Mommy goodbye, honey. We're going to see Aunt Kate."

"Her sister, so who knows when we'll get home." Bob Drew simulated idle chatter by tapping his forefinger and thumb together. "Women!" he complained as if Lacey didn't belong to the club. "They get together, and it's yap, yap, yap."

"Some men like to talk," Lacey said defensively. "My dad says he believes in keeping the lines of communication open. We just spent the day together and he did lots of talking." She didn't give a hoot if she sounded like a prig. Bob Drew badly needed educating.

He gave her a look that implied she had lost her mind, and turned his attention to his son instead. "Bye, champ," he said. "Tomorrow I'll be the Tin Man again, and you can be the Scarecrow."

"I want to be Toto," said Jason.

"It's kind of a small part," his father said doubtfully.

"I'm a good barker." Jason executed a series of loud barks. "See?"

Karen Drew held her ears. "Very authentic, honey. We'll be back around eleven," she said to Lacey, adding pointedly, "All that female yapping takes time, you know."

"Have fun." Lacey closed the door with her customary

feeling of relief. The parents were gone, and she and Jason could relax at last and begin their normal activities.

But Jason was so relaxed that he fell asleep on the couch by seven-thirty. Lacey looked down affectionately at the tousled head on her lap. He was loved as a baby, he was loved as a little boy. Even Bob Drew, the father she wouldn't wish on her worst enemy, played Tin Man to his son's Scarecrow. She could see him now, all stiff and steely-eyed, with his arm outstretched, waiting for Jason to unrust him with the oil can. Jason loved his father despite his flaws. Children were like that. And his father certainly loved him back. She thought about Louisa, the question mark in her sister's belly. Louisa already had the love of one family, even though they were about to give her up, to lose her from their daily lives. They loved her—that was understood. Louisa would be loved twice over.

A rapping noise on the door to the apartment was so low above the din of the television that Lacey wasn't sure she had heard it. She muted the TV sound and waited. A second, more insistent knocking roused her from the couch.

"Who is it?" she said in hushed tones without opening the door.

"It's me," said a voice. "It's Rob."

"Rob?" Her heart made a knocking sound of its own as she swung open the door. "What are you doing here?"

"I called you as soon as I got home from work, and your mother said you were babysitting." He stood awkwardly in the doorway. "Can I come in? Just for a little while?"

Lacey stepped aside, and Rob entered the apartment, bringing with him the faint odor of pea soup and french fries. As though he could read her mind, he said, "I didn't even shower. I wanted to make sure we had enough time to talk, so I came right over."

"Sit down," said Lacey, waving him in the direction of the sofa before she realized that Jason was stretched out on half of it.

Rob smiled at her, whispering, "It seems like old times, doesn't it?"

She nodded, and when he asked her if she wanted him to carry Jason to bed, she nodded once more. Rob scooped up the little boy, who moaned softly and curled against him as if he were his father. "Good night, little Jase," Rob spoke out loud as he carried the boy to his bedroom.

"They have the same layout we do," said Rob when he returned. "I figured he'd have the small room like the one my parents gave me."

"I never knew your mother died," said Lacey, saying the first thing that came into her head.

"She died not too long after we moved in here," said Rob. His face slackened as a look of grief passed over it.

"I'm sorry," Lacey whispered. "I didn't mean to make you sad."

"She was the best," said Rob. "I was lucky to have her."

They sat down together on the sofa. Lacey shifted into the corner, feeling much more like a timid little girl than someone who had symbolically thrown Rob into the garbage can. Not to mention slam-dunking six rolls at his girlfriend Caroline. "My sister is pregnant," she blurted out, appalled at herself the moment the words left her mouth.

"Don't hold back," said Rob, grinning, but the look he gave her made her feel as though he expected her to continue, that he actually wanted to hear what she had to say.

"We've been talking about it all afternoon. What to do," said Lacey. She hurried on. "I mean, what Rosie wants to do."

"But it's all tied up with the family," said Rob.

"Right." Rob's green eyes were keen with understanding. She could feel them on her face, on her hair, scanning her own eyes and cheeks and neck. He didn't take them off her once. Lacey spoke again. "At first, Rosie was going to have an abortion. We went to the clinic, and they told us about our options. Her options." Lacey took a deep breath. "She hated that word. It's too nice a word, I think, for what she was going through. And then they told her she was anemic and we had to wait some more, and meanwhile we visited my new half sister, who's this amazing baby." Lacey paused. She hadn't given Rob a moment to respond, because she was afraid that she would hate what he had to say. What if he was outraged, and talked about murdering babies and about children's rights? What if he ran back to his apartment and returned waving a placard of a bloody fetus in her face? She was prepared to fight, no, better yet, she was ready to kick him straight out the door.

Rob didn't move a muscle. He waited expectantly for her to finish.

"Now she wants to have the baby and find a couple who can't have children and have an open adoption. Do you know what that is?"

"Yup," said Rob.

"What do you think?" said Lacey.

Rob hesitated. "I think love is love," he said at last.

Lacey sat quietly, digesting his answer. "But what does that mean?" she said.

Rob held his hand out to her and she placed her own hand in his, naturally, without even thinking about it. "The minute I saw you walk into the deli, you were the one. I mean, I'd seen you in choir and in the hallway and stuff, but when you came in with that creep, what's his name . . ." Rob put a hand over Lacey's mouth. "No, Lace, you don't have to tell me, I know. Anyway, where was I?"

"When I came in with that creep, what's his name, whose name I don't have to tell you."

"Oh, right." He smiled. "When you drank that cup of coffee that you obviously hated . . ."

"You knew?"

Rob threw back his head and laughed. "I thought you were the cutest thing I'd ever seen." His face colored, and he looked down at the hand resting in his. "Why am I saying this? Oh, yeah. My mother. My mother told me that when she first saw me in Wakefield, that's the home I ended up in when my parents died, she said she was totally hooked."

"You were adopted?"

"Yeah. I mean, I don't know what I must have looked like then. I was skinny and scrawny, a pretty funny-looking six-year-old with these big Mickey Mouse ears that stuck out. I wore a baseball cap that my mother had bought for me, and I wouldn't take it off for the longest time."

"I'll bet you were adorable."

"I doubt it. But she said she loved me from the moment she laid eyes on me in that hat. When she and my father took me home, they let me wear it to bed. Wakefield never let me do that. And that's why I said 'love is love.'" He cleared his throat. "Your sister's baby will find lots of love, just like I did."

His eyes met hers with a look so raw and vulnerable that it took her breath away.

"Do you know what I mean?" he said.

"I think so," said Lacey. "But . . ."

"But what?"

"But what about Caroline?"

Rob squinted his eyes at her. "Are you crazy or something? The other day, when you got locked out, we felt something, didn't we? And you march into the deli and give my father your order and you take one look . . ."

"Jake is your father?"

"Yes, Jake is my father, I thought you knew that. And I'm in the back showing Caroline the kitchen because she wants a part-time job, and before I can speak, you're flying out the door!"

"She wants to work there?" said Lacey in a small voice.

"She does."

"You had your arm on her."

Rob chuckled. "I'm a friendly kind of guy, all right?"

"No, it's not all right," said Lacey huffily.

"Blondes aren't my type."

"Good," she answered, granting him a grin at last. "I was ready to run out and get the Clairol."

"Never change." Rob leaned over and kissed her gently on the lips. He smelled like french fries as he brushed her cheek with his and drew back. She had hated the smell of cream soda forevermore after Charles Pincer had kissed her. Lacey's smile was radiant as she looked at Rob. She would always love the aroma of french fries.

The house was dark by the time she got home, except for a light that her mother had left on in the hallway. Her father's car was gone, and so was her grandmother's.

Lacey walked into the kitchen. It was scrubbed clean and shining, the work of her grandmother. She opened the refrigerator and poured herself some seltzer, circling the kitchen as she drank it. She rinsed off her glass and placed it in the dish drainer. Behind it, sparkling in a corner, was a bowl of gaudy rings that her grandmother had forgotten.

She mounted the stairs slowly, scuffing each sneaker on the worn carpet. At the top of the steps, she could hear her mother snoring. Lacey slowly opened the bedroom door and peered into the darkness. Leonora's burnished red hair was spread across the pillow, her hand resting on her cheek. She looked like a teenager.

Rosie slept more quietly. Lacey leaned inside the bedroom door and watched the rise and fall of her sister's daisy-printed coverlet. She looked like a teenager. Someday soon, she would be a mother.

Lacey wandered into her room and sat on the side of the bed. She took off her sweatshirt, ran her fingers through her hair. Then she lay down on the bed and brought the shirt up to her face. It smelled of french fries. It pleased her. After all, love was love.